THE MAGIC SUITCASE 2

INTO THE LIGHT

by

John Behardien

Duncurin Publishing

Duncurin.com

This is a work of Fiction.
Available in Paperback and e-Book.

First Published in England MMXX

Duncurin Publishing
Monton
England

Duncurin.com

ISBN : 978-1-9162845-3-1

Book Design : Moosey.

DEDICATION

Harry! Had to be!

To Lisa

with Best Wishes

John Bebardien x

WITH THANKS

My sincere thanks to the following very talented people.

Amelia Phythian for some fabulous illustrations. Amelia.phythian@gmail.com

Copy Edit. Sarah at Bookhelpline.co.uk

Other Images iStockPhoto.com "Yangna"

Other Books By John Behardien

Crack In the Code
Stars' End

The Last Great Gift

Dawn Over Vancouver
All That Time Allows

Final Horizon
Final Request
Final Truth

One Life Many Moments

The Magic Suitcase – from Age 9
The Magic Suitcase II, Into The Light – from Age 12
The Magic Suitcase Saves Christmas – from Age 5

CONTENTS

Chapter I

The Girl

Mary looked in the rear-view mirror as she drove and the rubbish-tip receded into the background. She was just able to see the black handle of the old suitcase above the back seat where it lay in the boot of the car. She looked at Piper, her daughter, after glancing irritatedly to the roof-lining, seeking more reserves of patience.

Mary sighed. "I can't believe that we've just brought back an old suitcase from the tip. It looks like the sort of thing that someone takes to the tip and leaves there!"

"Well Mum, you heard what that young boy, Tommy, and his friend said. He said it would help us within a few days. Why don't we see what happens over the next couple of days?"

"Very well. But once we've shown how foolish and gullible we both are, *you* can take it back to the tip. I bet they're both having a good laugh at *our* expense right now. For heaven's sake!" She shook her head from side to side. "It's just an old red case that's seen better days and belongs at the tip!"

"I will, Mum," Piper said, but added quietly, "I thought they both seemed genuine."

Her mum made a noise that was half way between a laugh and a scoff. It wasn't difficult to pick up on her mood. She'd been like this for weeks; in fact, ever since Piper's dad had left. Nor was it difficult to see the pain, the betrayal, and yes, the anger, on her face. These, without doubt, were emotions that Piper shared, and yet her dad was her dad. Surely, she could only ever have one dad, imperfect though he might be. Piper knew that her mum had no one else to talk to, and she reasoned that now was the time to make sure that her mum had no such doubts about her.

She'd been badly let down, that was for sure, and it was time to not only be a good listener, but also to stand by her.

"I will, Mum, I promise," was meant to convey so much more than the simple words could.

"And, I'm not having that *thing* in the house." Mary looked again in her rear-view mirror as if she was talking directly to the case and not to Piper, "It can go in the garage…on its way to the tip."

"Okay then, Mum. I'll make sure about that too."

"Oh, and I wish you'd get that hair cut."

Piper grabbed a bunch of soft blonde, but unruly, hair and smoothed it downwards as she gently pulled on it. "I like it like this. I know it's a bit long, but some girls would kill to have hair like mine."

"Well, it's untidy and needs a jolly good cut. And as for that fringe!"

"Okay, Mum, I'm sure it will need cutting before I go back to school in September."

Mary became quieter; she'd obviously voiced at least a couple of the things that were troubling her…for now! Piper knew there'd be more to come in the days to follow but she'd run out of comforting words and just had to leave her mum to the painful and negative thoughts that clearly still besieged her. Moreover, it was hard and tiring work just encouraging her mum to get through the day. In a measure of how bad things were at the moment, Piper couldn't wait for school to start in September, and it wasn't even August yet. She'd been tipped to get good grades in her GCSEs and was looking forward to starting Sixth Form College in a few weeks' time.

They reached the little semi-detached house at the end of the cul-de-sac. Mary left the car on the drive as usual, leaving Piper to open the boot and remove the case. As requested, she placed the case in the garage. She'd seen the way the two children, Tommy and Rosie, had stroked the top of it before they handed it over. She did the same now. It seemed that here and now, as she looked at the shabby case, faded except for its bright gold zips, her mum was right. How could it be anything other than an old case destined for the tip? Surely, it must be a joke, and the joke was on both her and her mum.

However, in the past few weeks they'd both learnt that nothing was as it seemed, and this had culminated in them losing so much and not just a husband and father. In truth, after losing just about everything, they had very little else to lose – or so they thought. Piper could only hope that the two children she'd met at the tip were correct and the case could help them. It seemed clear to her that nobody else would. She opened the garage door and put the case against the wall. Then she closed the up-and-over door and went inside the house. Her mum was lying on the sofa.

"Case is in the garage, Mum."

"Oh thanks, Piper. We can take it back to the tip in a day or two." Her mum yawned. "Oh my, I am so tired; I just can't keep my eyes open. I'm going to make an appointment with the doctor to see if he can give me a tonic or something. Must be all this business with your dad."

"I'll make you a cup of tea, Mum."

A few minutes later Piper went into the lounge with a cup of tea for her mum but she was fast asleep. Piper placed the mug of tea on the side table and went upstairs to do some reading in her room. Her footsteps on the stairs were laden with worry and fear over what was going to become of them both. Case or no case, Piper had a bad feeling about almost everything at the moment.

Chapter 2

Voice in the dark

A little while later, Mary called Piper down to have her tea. Her mum stirred at the food on her own plate but didn't really eat very much at all. Moreover, despite her sleep that afternoon she looked drained and exhausted.

Piper looked at her mum, the concern etched on her young face, "Are you okay, Mum?"

"I've made an appointment with the GP." Mary said defensively as if trying to deflect her daughter's alarm. "They had a cancellation and he can see me the day after tomorrow. I'm sure he'll be able to give a me a nice tonic to give me some more energy."

"Mum, you haven't eaten much. Could you not try eating a bit more?"

"Look, Piper, I can't face it. I'm sure the doctor will sort me out."

After a little more unsuccessful cajoling of her mother, Piper picked the plates up off the kitchen table and ran the water for the washing up. Her mum looked dreadful and she wondered if a tonic would be able to do much for her.

After their meal, they went into the lounge to watch a film. Despite it being one of her mum's favourites, Piper noticed that her mum had soon fallen asleep and although she would ask her later why she had not woken her, Piper realised that her mum needed the rest more than watching a film. That night, Piper sat reading in bed for a while before turning out her light. Despite worries over her mum that had been keeping her awake for the past week or two, she soon entered a deep sleep. A vivid dream came to her as she slept, one that in her deep sleep seemed very real, and yet it was one of which she would remember very little the following day.

In her dream, she couldn't see clearly because it was so dark. The most impactful feature of her dream, however, weren't the images but the voices; and one voice in particular! It seemed that a man was talking to someone else, but she could only hear one half of the conversation. This is what she heard:

"I know it's cold and dark in here. Maybe it will only be for a few days. I'm sure they'll move you into the house.

"Yes, I know, it's going to be very hard and it'll be touch and go. We promised, we said that she was going to be okay. We just have to do our best and hope it's enough.

"I know you are frightened and being in here doesn't help.

"Yes, I'm frightened too. It seems so hard but remember, we are their only hope. If we give up on them, then there's no one else.

"No, you're right, he isn't going to help them; neither of them.

"Yes, just do your best and with luck, we'll come through.

"Yes, I promise, do your best and I'll come for you. I'll ask Barney to stay with you until morning."

Piper stirred in her sleep. She turned and glanced at her alarm clock, and she thought she heard a man's voice say, "Be brave in here. Maybe tomorrow Piper will move you from this dark, cold place and into the light. Things will look so much better then, I promise. Barney, good boy, you stay here until I come for you. Good doggy."

Piper shook her head gently, she thought she'd heard a voice but it must have been a dream. She also thought she'd heard a bark from a large dog. She was asleep again by the time her head turned on the pillow.

Piper woke the following day. It was dry and sunny and after making herself and her mum some breakfast, she thought she'd go for a bike ride. She opened the garage. She saw the red suitcase by the wall where she'd left it the day before; its bright, gold zips seemed very dull in the shade of the garage. She went over to pat it in the way the two children from the tip had done. She got her bike and, after closing the door, rode off.

She cycled to the other side of town where they'd built the new executive estate. No two of the large detached houses were alike and yet all of them featured the massive white-painted gables that were illuminated at night, and the columned porticos, of artificial stone, that were set above the substantial wooden double doors that made up the front entrances. Piper stared at the sight for some time. Surely, such vast edifices of brick, stone and timber had come to typify the rich, the successful and, without doubt, those that were content. Perhaps the speed with which the new development had sold out underlined the aspirations of those new owners.

On one sweeping block drive, before the triple garage were parked two expensive motor cars. She recognised the blue one – the Porsche – straight away: it was her father's. Its poise readily apparent as it gleamed in the sunshine.

Piper stopped over the road, still a little distance away, and as she watched, she saw the front door open. She quickly hid as much of herself as she could behind one of the bushes in the garden opposite; the end of her bike was still clearly visible as she clung to it. A young blonde woman appeared from the house. She was tall and slim and she skipped along lightly in her gorgeous heels. From her hand-sewn handbag, she withdrew a key fob and clicked at the other car. It responded instantly and she opened the driver's door as the wind caught her hem just enough to reveal her shapely legs. She waved back at the house to the person who was now standing on the front step. He pulled his dressing gown around his body more tightly as the wind approached him and waved back excitedly. Piper recognised her father. Most notably, she saw the sheer happiness that existed on his face; such happiness she'd never seen him display when he was at home with them.

Piper remained there for a few minutes, transfixed by the scene, even after the car had driven away with a roar from the throaty multiple exhausts and a squeal from the fat tyres.

The woman in the house facing detected some movement through the glass front door and opened it to find a young woman hiding behind the bush in her front garden. She was about to ask the girl what she was doing but as the young woman turned, she saw her tear-stained face. Rather than admonish her, she elected simply to ask her if she was all right. Piper nodded as she used her palm to sweep away at least some of the tears. She nodded again, tried her best to smile and managed to force out a nasal sounding 'thank you' before riding off.

After about half an hour of riding, punctuated by a few more tears, Piper reached home. She opened the garage door but even with more light coming in, it remained cold and dark in there. She brushed past the suitcase as she placed her bike against the wall and noticed that protruding from the uppermost pocket of the suitcase was an envelope. She grabbed the envelope and made for the door. She reached up and was about to pull it closed but then she remembered a fragment of a dream that she'd otherwise largely forgotten. She went back for the case and dragged it out of the dark, cold garage and into the light. As if to encourage her, a shaft of warm sunlight chose that very moment to pierce the clouds that had drifted in and illuminate much of the cul-de-sac where they lived.

She took the case inside and placed it against the wall in the hallway with its laminate floor that was lifting around the edges. Her mum was sitting at the little table in the kitchen, watching.

"Why have you brought the case in? I thought it was to stay in the garage."

"It's cold and dark in there, Mum. I thought it would be better inside with us."

Her mum laughed, "Look, Piper, it's just an old suitcase. It's not alive, it doesn't have feelings and I'm pretty certain those kids were playing a bit of a prank on us. I'm thinking that you'll be taking it back to the tip in a day or two."

Suddenly, her mum recoiled in horror as a large spider crawled from the lower front pocket. Piper grabbed a clear plastic cup from the shelf that she reserved for such eventualities. She covered the spider, slipped a handy piece of card under the cup and opened the front door to eject the creature outside.

"I hate those things and you hate them too. Why don't you just stamp on them?"

"Well, Mum, I guess it will be much better outside rather than being squashed under my trainers. As for the case, I promise I'll take it back in a day or two if nothing happens."

"Trust me, nothing is going to happen."

"Oh, look, Mum, I found this on the case. It's addressed to Dr Bodger. Is that the GP you are booked to see tomorrow?"

"What, a letter? How did it get here? And it's addressed to my GP. Do you think the postman delivered it by mistake?"

Piper told her mum that she didn't know what to think, and yet something stirred within. Those two children at the tip had seemed sincere and deadly serious. Maybe they had really passed on a magic case, just as they said. Her thoughts moved on; surely it was just a simple letter and how could this be of any importance whatsoever. She laughed to herself, but placed the case in the hallway next to the radiator nonetheless. The summer sun streamed in through the glazed front door and the golden zips gave off a bright shimmer as they reflected the light that now flooded in. More than this, Piper found herself patting the case every time she passed it in the hall.

"I'm so tired, Piper, I think I'll go for a lie down. You can make yourself a sandwich if you are hungry."

Mary was still in bed when Piper called her to see if she'd like to have some tea. Piper had taken a frozen meal out of the freezer and microwaved this together with some vegetables of uncertain age. As the young girl had looked in the freezer and the cupboards, she'd noticed that there was very little food in the house.

Once again, her mum moved the food round on her plate but ate very little. Piper looked at her mum with some concern. Mary caught her gaze.

"I have this appointment tomorrow. You see, I'll be as right as rain in no time."

Piper gave an involuntary shiver and wondered what could possibly be right with rain.

Chapter 3

The Appointment

Dr Bodger looked at his patient a little absent-mindedly. He kept repeating her name in the hope that, somehow, this would bring more information to bear. Sadly, even with many repetitions of her name, the slightly startled look persisted upon his expression.

Mary sensed his thoughts and offered a little clarification as she kept nodding slowly in his direction to assist him further, "Mary Milton, Doctor Bodger. I don't come very often. I'm here because I've been feeling so tired of late. My husband has just left me and my daughter. I'm sure it's to do with this. I was wondering about a tonic or something to give me some energy." She hoped that by repeating this summary for him at least once, it would spur him into action.

Dr Bodger nodded as if a management plan had just come to him, "So, do you want some pills? Perhaps, some antidepressants? They are not bad. Take them myself from time to time and look at me."

What little of Mary's confidence that still remained in the GP evaporated like a droplet of water contacting a glowing hob.

"Well, I was wondering about a tonic, perhaps. Something to get me feeling a bit stronger and less tired."

Dr Bodger looked at his patient a little quizzically but sadly he missed her pale features and the slightly yellow tinge to her complexion.

"A tonic? Yes, I'm sure that's a good idea. A *tonic* it is. I'll just print out a prescription for you and I'm sure you'll be feeling better in no time. Now, a tonic? A tonic, you say, let me see." Once again he looked uncertain. "I'll just look in my book here for a suitable one to give you. You sure you don't want antidepressants?" She shook her head slowly as he picked up a well-thumbed copy of the book on his desk, which contained a list of all the things that were available for him to prescribe. Mary noted that the book naturally seemed to fall open on the section marked 'antidepressants'.

Mary looked down at her handbag. She saw the letter that she'd placed there that morning.

"Oh, Dr Bodger, this came for you."

"Came? Came where?"

"To my house. I think the postman must have made a mistake as it's addressed to you."

"To me? To your house? How did that happen?"

"Well, I'm not sure, but here it is." She handed over the letter.

"What's in it, then?"

"Well, I don't know. It was sealed. Perhaps *you* should open it?" Mary suggested, sensing that they weren't getting very far.

He produced a long and pointed letter knife, which he held with a flourish a bit like a musketeer in an episode of brave derring-do. Mary jumped back a little at the speed of his movement.

The GP opened the letter and fished out a form. "My, my, it's one of ours and it's made out in your name. That's curious. To your *house*, you say?"

She nodded, but didn't speak as she suddenly felt even more tired. Dr Bodger seemed completely stumped by the form as he held it up and stared at it. Eventually, words stirred: "Well, that's a good idea, I suppose."

"What is it, Doctor?"

"A blood test," he offered with a further flourish as the surprise at what he'd found subsided. "That's what you *need*." He pointed to the form, "It's for a few tests. This test, that test and another test," as his words became more and more vague as if he'd never heard of any of the tests that were ticked on the form.

"Of course, it will take me *ages* to get a blood appointment for you. I'd do it myself, only the mince pies aren't what they used to be."

"Mince pies, Doctor?" she asked just as he looked at his large wristwatch a little myopically.

"Yes, you know, 'eyes'." Mary nodded.

"I'll book you in with Nurse Smooth. It'll be a week or two, though." He looked uncertainly at his computer screen as if he'd never seen it before in his life and what information it displayed was a constant surprise to him. "Well, upon my soul! She has an appointment in *five* minutes and, and you have been booked into it. Did you phone ahead, two weeks ago, perhaps?"

"Not me, Doctor."

"Ah well, if you'd go and sit on her chair, she'll do it for you now. Did you want some pills while you are here?"

"Could we perhaps wait for the results, Doctor? Would that be all right?"

"Very well then, and then we can give you some pills or maybe a nice tonic, was it? Or did we decide on some antidepressants?" Mary nodded and got up as quickly as her tiredness allowed. Moreover, she was grateful when Dr Bodger looked with some confusion at his screen again, as if it was all very new, and told her that Nurse Smooth was now ready. Mary left his consulting room quickly, sought out Nurse Smooth, had her blood test and then went home.

Piper was quizzing her mum over a cup of tea in their small kitchen with the square table. "So, Dr Bodger hadn't sent the blood test, Mum?"

"No, in fact, he looked as though he'd never seen a blood test ever before!"

"Oh well, I suppose it was good that he did some tests."

Mary nodded but both mother and daughter had departed into their own thoughts; Mary worrying about her blood test and Piper wondering if the red suitcase had had something to do with a blood form and appointment suddenly appearing. The young woman thought she'd better keep her own counsel – for now at least. Her mum wasn't ready to accept that there could possibly be anything either good or magical about the case in the hallway.

The following day, the phone rang and as Piper answered, the gentleman on the line seemed a little agitated. "Ah yes, hello, is that Mary, Mary Milton?"

"No, it's Piper, her daughter. Do you want to speak to her?"

"Oh, yes please."

Piper went to find her mother; she was lying on the sofa.

"Mum, it's a call for you."

Mary came to the phone, "Hello," she began.

"Now Mary, it's Dr Bodger here. I wonder if you could call in this afternoon, to the surgery as I need to discuss your blood test with you?"

"Oh yes, what time would be convenient for you, Doctor? Nothing serious, I hope.

"I'm thinking it's nothing we can't fix, Mary. How is 2 pm for you?"

"That's fine, I'll see you then, Doctor"

"Mum, was that Dr Bodger?"

"Yes, he says he wants to see me. Nothing to worry about."

A shiver coursed its way through Piper's body. She had a bad feeling about the call, about Dr Bodger, and just about all of it. "Do you mind if I come with you, Mum?"

"I'm sure that isn't necessary, Piper."

"Please, Mum."

"Very well then, if you insist, but I am sure it's just routine."

"Oh, I'm sure it is," she agreed, trying to place more certainty on her words than she could feel within.

Dr Bodger met them both at the consulting room door.

"Dr Bodger, this is my daughter, Piper."

"Yes, hello Piper. Please take a seat both of you. Look, Mary, it's about your blood test. I'm afraid you have a blood disorder: a rare form of leukaemia."

Both Mary and Piper looked horrified.

"Now then, I'm sure we'll soon sort it out. I'll refer you in the next few days and you'll get an appointment from my friend and medical school buddy, Dr Ivor Habandon. He's a specialist at the local District General hospital. You see, he'll see you in a couple of weeks and I'm sure he'll have you back on track in no time."

"Is that not serious, Dr Bodger?" asked Piper.

"Oh no, I'm sure that's not the case. We'll soon have it under control and my old friend is a super physician. He's a *consultant*, you know."

"Doesn't Mum need to see a blood specialist, Doctor? Maybe someone urgently?"

"Now, now, young lady you leave it all to me. I'm the professional here and I know what needs to be done and how quickly. Just look out for a letter. It will be posted in due course to your home."

Neither of the two women looked the slightest bit reassured.

"Do I not need to be referred *urgently*, Doctor?" Mary asked after picking up on the alarm etched on her daughter's face.

Dr Bodger laughed, “Oh no, don’t worry! My pal will see you soon enough and have you sorted. Tell you what, I’ll dictate the letter myself and my secretary will have it in the post in no time to Dr Habandon.

“Oh, very well then, Doctor, I’ll wait for it to come through.”

Both left the consulting room. Piper remained most unhappy.

“Mum, I have a bad feeling here. Surely this is serious and don’t you think Dr…Dr…Bodger should be treating it as such?”

“You heard him, Piper, I’m sure if it were serious, he’d have said so. We have to trust him, you know. I’m sure he knows what he is doing.”

Piper couldn’t see this. She couldn’t see this at all. Furthermore, she’d seen the way her mum was deteriorating. She seemed worse by the day. She could only think that Dr Bodger had underestimated just how poorly her mum was. Piper decided as soon as they got home to do some internet research about Dr Ivor Habandon.

Chapter 4

Wires Crossed

After Mary and Piper had gone, Dr Bodger dictated a letter to his colleague and friend, Dr Habandon. He placed the dictation tape on the 'routine' pile on his secretary's desk who was on her break. A short time later, she returned to her somewhat chaotic desk. She looked at the pile of tapes on her desk. It had been a busy day but most of the tapes were routine and would wait until she returned from her week-long holiday that she planned to take the following week. Only two were urgent and these tapes had been placed in the appropriate tray on top of her desk, so marked. She swivelled round on her chair in order to put some paper in her printer. Somehow, her foot had become caught in the flex that ran under her desk. She didn't know how this had happened but the wire, which ran over the desk to the dictation machine at the back, pulled both trays containing the tapes on to the floor. She looked down quickly. She was sure that the tape that she picked up was one of those from the 'urgent' tray. She began typing straight away, marking the letter 'Urgent' as she always did, with those from that tray, and then typed in the patient details.

'Mary Milton, 10, Crossview Drive…'

A couple of minutes later she'd finished the letter and printed a copy for the patient file.

She went over to the fax machine in order to fax it to Dr Habandon at the local hospital. She knew the numbers off by heart as they referred most of their cases to him. He was an old chum of Dr Bodger and one way or another most of their referrals ended up going to him. She knew his details so well, in fact, she could even type in the numbers without looking. She began typing on the keypad and then realised that she wasn't alone. She looked through the window and was surprised to find a very large Alsatian staring at her. Although she was on the ground floor, her office window was fairly small and she reasoned that not only would the dog have to be standing on his back paws but he would also have to be a big dog to be able to reach this height. He stood there for a moment or two, his fluffy ears had pricked up as if he were interested in what she was doing and his head angled to the side. She looked away for a second, continued keying the numbers very quickly despite her distraction and the paper was drawn into the machine as it dialled out and connected. The urgent fax was on its way. She looked back to the window but the dog had disappeared.

At the point of destination, another fax machine beeped, and it began printing within a second or two. Monica Blaize looked at the fax. She was a little confused because although the fax was addressed to Dr Habandon at the smaller District General Hospital, some miles away, it appeared to have come to exactly the right person and the right place. She took the fax from the machine and carried it next door to her boss' office. She tapped lightly on the door marked 'Dr Phil Brill, Specialist in Haematology.' Dr Brill looked up from reading some of the papers sprawled over his desk.

Monica began, "Dr Brill, this fax has just come through. It's addressed to Dr Habandon at the DGH, but it looks like it's really intended for you as it mentions your specialty, Leukaemia."

"Oh, yes indeed, Monica, I can see what you mean. I think they must have thought better of involving Dr Habandon as he wouldn't have been able to deal with this. He is more of a general physician and not a blood specialist." He looked at the blood results that had been sent with the fax. He didn't like what he saw. "Good job they sent it to us as we need to see this lady urgently. Could I ask you…?"

There was a pause but Monica was already reaching for the fax with the patient details. "Yes, of course, Doctor, I'll phone the lady, Mrs Milton, straight away and get her in to see you tomorrow?"

He smiled, "Yes, wonderful, as always. It cuts out a lot of unnecessary words, you being able to read my mind."

"That's my pleasure, Doctor Brill. I'll ask the lady to come down tomorrow."

Dr Brill thought aloud as he considered his new patient. "It's such a shame the recent trial has just finished. She'd have been ideal for the trial drug and we'll never get the Health Trust to agree to funding more patients now that we've reached the target number. Not that we'd ever be able to get our hands on more supplies anyway!"

"Yes, I suppose they'd remind you that the trial drug costs £100,000 a week!"

He nodded sadly and she went to phone their new patient.

Piper had just come downstairs. She planned to find her mother and have a long talk with her. Dr Bodger had referred her to Dr Habandon and it seemed he was a generalist. Piper's online searches had revealed that her mum needed to see a specialist, at least a blood specialist, and then preferably one with a special interest in leukaemia. Just as she went through the hallway, the phone rang.

"Good afternoon, is that Mary Milton?"

"No, it's Piper, her daughter. She is lying down; shall I get her?"

Monica paused, judging by the concerned look upon Dr Brill's face, the poor lady was clearly very ill. She decided that there was no time to lose and gave the daughter the information.

"Oh, my name is Monica and I am secretary to Dr Phil Brill. Your mum has been referred to him urgently with a blood disorder."

"Dr Brill? We were told that Dr Habandon would be writing to us. Does Dr Brill specialise in blood disorders?"

"Yes, very much so. He is one of the country's leading specialists in this field. We are based at St Catherine's Hospital which is the regional centre. I'm afraid it's a few miles for you and it's too late for me to book an ambulance. If your mum is able to travel, we'd like her here for 10 am, please."

Piper did a little dance while still holding on to the phone.

"Hello, are you still there?"

"Oh yes, many thanks. It's so kind of you to phone. We'll be there tomorrow."

"That's wonderful. Please come to Block C. Dr Brill's clinic is there."

"Thank you, Monica, we'll be there tomorrow. Thanks again for your call.

Piper went to have a chat with her mum.

"Mum, we'll need to get a taxi. It's ten miles to St Catherine's"

"What? What happened to Dr Habandon at the hospital down the road?"

"Look, Mum, this chap, Dr Brill is a *super* specialist. This is the man you need, to get you well again."

"A taxi will cost a fortune."

"I'll get on to the taxi firm first thing. Mum, look, we need this; you need this."

"I'm sorry, Piper, I haven't been able to find a job and feeling so tired hasn't helped. I'm not sure we can afford a taxi. You know your dad's been a bit…a bit forgetful; maybe he's distracted."

"I know Mum. He'll get round to us, I'm sure."

Piper didn't voice what they both knew but neither had said. He had received a significant promotion at work, one that came with a massive rise in his salary and allowances. At first, it had seemed like a dream come true and then he started working late. Then he said he would have to work some weekends. Some became all; there were more absences from the family home and then one day he didn't return at all, simply texting his wife that their marriage of twenty years was over.

Piper nodded. She had some money that her aunt in Canada had sent her for her forthcoming birthday, her sixteenth. She'd use that for the taxi if need be, but there was no way her mum was going to miss that appointment, even if Piper had to carry her there on her back. She took the fifty Canadian Dollars from her money box and went up to the local post office to see if they could change it into sterling.

The following day, Piper clicked on the taxi app on her phone. It told her that their taxi driver was on his way and would be arriving in a blue Ford. In point of fact, a white car appeared and a short elderly gentleman got out of the car. His large tummy got in the way a bit and he had to struggle to get himself past the steering wheel, which he eventually did with a bit of a chuckle and an accusatory pat to his middle. He told the two women that he'd been sent by the hospital and he would be taking them there in time for their appointment. Piper moved quickly to cancel the taxi on her App but noticed that it had disappeared. Maybe, the blue Ford driver had answered another call.

Mary slipped into the back seat after the driver held the door open for her. Piper got in through the other rear door.

"Thank you for collecting us. You say you are employed by the hospital?"

"That I am, Ma'am, my name is Brett."

Mary looked at the balding elderly gentleman with the ample tummy. He wore a bright-red check flannel shirt stuffed into an old belt, which just about made the distance around his middle and also held up a pair of blue corduroy trousers that had seen better days. More than this, Mary had noticed that the material was shiny over his bottom, presumably from him spending much of the day driving.

Brett checked that his passengers were seated and that they'd both found their seatbelts. He closed the rear door with a chuckle as he grabbed his own door.

"Brett? Forgive me, but you look more like a Percy or maybe a Walter or even a Vernon."

"He hey, a lot of folk say that," he replied, as he looked at Mary in the rear-view mirror, and then Piper could have sworn that she heard him mumble that he would perhaps try one of those names next. Even more impactful, was the fact that the young woman thought she'd heard his voice before but just couldn't place it or him.

"Are you local, Brett?" Mary asked.

"No, not really, Madam."

"You don't sound local."

"A lot of folk say that as well!"

"Ah well, it's so kind of you to arrive in this way."

We were told that there wasn't enough time to book an ambulance," interjected Piper, quickly, sensing that her mum was in danger of insulting the old chap.

He chuckled to himself as if he'd picked up on her thoughts. "Oh yes, that's right, Miss. I fill those gaps when urgent appointments are arranged. I'll soon have you both there. I'm told Dr Brill is the best there is."

Piper nodded and for a second wondered how he knew which specialist they were attending but then decided that the hospital must give him a schedule each morning of collections and transfers. She looked over at her mum with concern. Just those few words had tired her and she looked very pale and wan. Piper had a feeling that all of Dr Brill's skills were going to be needed, since her mum looked even worse today.

Brett dropped them just outside Dr Brill's clinic and there was only a short distance to the waiting room. The receptionist asked them to take a seat and the specialist would be with them shortly. Mary was panting a little as she sat in the chair; the short walk enough to bring on her discomfort.

Dr Brill lived up to his name. He was kind, thorough and explained in detail what was wrong with Mary and what treatment he planned to put in place. He paced up and down the room a little as if he needed more time to think or if he'd forgotten something, but he was clear that he would do everything in his power to treat his patient and achieve a favourable outcome.

"I am sorry, Mary, you know from what I've told you that this is very serious. This being said, I am an expert in this field and have been treating patients like you for many years. We plan to start chemotherapy next week and it's a fairly intensive treatment course that we have planned. We will need to see you tomorrow afternoon for some more blood tests and to look at your bone marrow. You'll spend a day a week with us and we'll get you home, if we can, after each session."

Both Mary and Piper had questions for their specialist and he did his best to answer each and every one of them in detail. After their appointment, they found that Brett was waiting for them to take them home.

Piper clutched at her phone; she'd been about to summon her taxi App. "Oh wow! We didn't realise you'd be able to take us back as well."

"My pleasure Miss, It's all part of the service we provide. I'll even collect you tomorrow in good time for your afternoon appointment."

Once again, Piper was surprised. Brett must know that this was the way that Dr Brill's clinic worked. She could only think that Brett must be a very experienced driver.

As they drove away, Dr Brill dictated his notes and spoke with Zoe his nurse. He shook his head gravely, " I am afraid Mary is very poorly. It's going to be touch and go." He sighed as he looked at her notes, "She would have been ideal for the new treatment drug. It's such a shame we've used our full allocation."

Zoe nodded. She recognised the look that he gave her: one of part regret and part fear. Such a look always came before a dreadful outcome. They hadn't lost many patients since the new drug trial but this was now over and she knew that, just like they were for her, the faces and the names of those who had been unlucky were forever etched upon Dr Brill's every waking moment.

Mary and Piper arrived home a short while later. They thanked their driver who wished them well, assured them that the service was completely free and with another chuckle, jumped back in his car, then squeezed his tummy past the steering wheel and drove off.

Chapter 5

Sixteen Summers

The following day it was Piper's birthday; it was her sixteenth. She came down fairly early and made herself some breakfast. There were no presents and when the postman pushed the post through the letterbox, there were no cards either. Even worse was the fact that by now Piper had learned to recognise the stiff formality of those envelopes – the ones that had been delivered – 'advising' on the consequences of the unpaid bills that she knew had been slowly building since her dad had left.

Piper knew that if her mum had been well, she'd have bought her at least a card. She could see now that over the years her dad had promised much but delivered little and it must have been her mum who had always done her best to make sure that their daughter had a card and a present to open. This was the saddest thing of all. Her mum's illness and difficulties with money had precluded her from getting out to the shops and much, if not all, of her spending. Piper realised that her mum was now unable to do the things that she had always done – things which, no doubt, year on year, her dad had either forgotten or had simply not bothered to do.

Not that Piper was surprised by this as it was simply a brutal reminder that her dad had moved on even before his absence from their lives and she, like her mum, was nothing but old baggage that had been left behind like a limping donkey who was no longer of any use to a traveller.

Mary got up a little while later but she looked very pale and very weak. She looked unsteady on her feet as she walked.

"Happy birthday, my love. Look, I am sorry I didn't get you anything. As soon as I am feeling better, I will get you something; I promise."

Piper noticed that just speaking a few words had made her mum short of breath.

"Oh, don't worry, Mum. There'll be plenty of time for presents when you are better," she said, whilst trying to display more confidence than she could feel within.

In her sixteen years, she'd never not received any presents…and she had never seen anyone who looked as poorly as her mum.

"I take it your dad didn't send you anything?"

"I'm sure he's busy, Mum; maybe in a day or two."

Mary smiled but did her best not to reveal any of her innermost thoughts. This was typical of Piper: she always tried to look on the brighter side of her life and was never quick to think bad thoughts about anyone, not even her dad who surely deserved such treatment. Mercifully, her pale, sallow complexion just about hid the look of betrayal that would otherwise have been obvious.

Piper thought she heard something in the hallway and went to look. As she did so, she bumped into the red suitcase that had rolled a little further away from the wall. It was at this point that she noticed something protruding from the lower zipped compartment that was gaping open. She withdrew a long slim parcel that was beautifully wrapped with a large bow in pink ribbon tied around its middle. She carried it back to the kitchen where her mum had sat down and held it up for her mum's inspection.

She pointed to the nicely wrapped box and as she did so her right eyebrow raised with excitement and curiosity as she said, "It's addressed to me! It was poking out from the suitcase!"

Mary laughed. "Go on open it. I am fascinated; let's have a look."

Piper unwrapped the present to reveal a long oblong box. She opened this up and showed her mum the contents.

"Mum, GHDs! These are the top-of-the-range ones with the new ceramic plates. At last, I can straighten my hair properly and I won't have to have it cut."

"Well, I think you should still get it cut but at least it will look a lot tidier. What a fabulous present. Say, do you think your dad left them?"

"No, Mum, I don't honestly think he'd know what they were, let alone that I needed a pair of straighteners just like them."

"So who then?" Mary looked at her daughter. "Don't say that case, please!"

Piper just smiled and shrugged her shoulders. She knew that her mum remained deeply sceptical of the case. Mary could interpret the look on Piper's face; she knew that she was carefully managing her words and especially with regard to the case.

"So, go on then, do you think this is the first piece of magic from the case?"

"Perhaps," began Piper carefully, but then she became quiet as she thought that they both had the case to thank for the blood test request, even before considering the straighteners.

Her mum saw her shiver. Piper couldn't help but wonder what would have become of her mum if the blood test had not taken place. Furthermore, she believed that Dr Bodger would have taken a long, long time before suggesting such a thing. Another fact that puzzled the young woman was how quickly the referral had been acted upon and how the hospital and consultant had changed. She could only think that Dr Habandon had read the letter and, sensing that it was not his area of expertise, had sent it straight through to Dr Brill. How fortunate that he had done so. At the back of her mind, however, came the lingering thought that it was possible that Dr Habandon had, mysteriously, been bypassed completely.

Piper looked at the GHDs and held them up as they almost gleamed in her hand. "I'll be down in a minute, Mum. I'm going to try out my new straighteners." With this, she ran upstairs to her room to find her brush and plug them in.

That afternoon Brett arrived in the white car to take Mary and her daughter to the hospital.

"Oh hello, Brett, nice to see you again."

The elderly driver held the door open for Mary.

"Look, Piper, you'll be stuck with me all afternoon. You can stay here if you like and I'm sure Brett will be able to bring me back when we've finished. If not, I can get a taxi."

The elderly driver nodded and chuckled to himself whilst somehow managing to say that it would be his pleasure.

"Oh, no. No you don't. I'm coming with you. Someone has to keep an eye on you."

Brett chuckled again and, after making sure that they were both seated, he drove to the hospital.

The marrow tests were painful, but Dr Brill once again lived up to his name. After a few hours, Mary and Piper were ready for home. Brett waited for them.

"Brett, it's so kind of you to ferry us about in this way. Are you sure we can't pay you for your time or your petrol?"

"Oh no, Ma'am, it's my job to ferry poorly folk about in this way. The hospital pay me my wages and it's my job."

"Well, I'd like you to know how grateful I am."

Brett nodded as Mary said this and a few minutes later they arrived at the small house in the quiet cul-de-sac.

"I'll see you ladies, next week."

"Oh Brett, thank you so much."

As soon as they opened the front door, Mary saw an important letter was waiting for them. It was from the mortgage company. She immediately tried to hide it but Piper had already seen the envelope with its seals and barcodes. She guessed even before her mum spoke that it was not good news. In truth, she'd been expecting such a letter as she also knew that her mum had received no support from her father and crucially, there was little money coming in and a steady stream of bills continued to fall due.

Piper soon came to a conclusion. "Mum, lots of my friends have summer jobs. I'm sure I will be able to get something, and my wages can help out until you are better and we are on our feet more."

"That's kind of you, Piper. Maybe I can have a word with your dad to see if he can help us out."

The following day, Piper walked up to the main street to see if any part-time jobs were available. She managed to get a few hours at the local bakery but it meant starting work at 5 am. She did her utmost to keep a straight face while she told her mum that she was looking forward to the early starts and assured her that the summer days and weather would make it so much easier.

Mary had left several messages with her ex-husband on his mobile phone but none of her calls were returned. She knew that the mortgage lender was now getting very restless and, although Piper was doing her best, it was unlikely that with her meagre wages they would be able to hold them off for much longer. Even without taking into account her illness, Mary knew that her financial situation had ventured well beyond critical and she was forced to contemplate which, if any, of the few people she knew would be able to put them up once they were evicted from their home. Her only course of action now would be to put the house on the market as soon as possible. In any event, if she did nothing, the lender would sell the house from right under them and no doubt be happy to entertain the lowest of offers provided the loan was paid off – leaving Mary with nothing.

The following afternoon, Piper came in from work. She looked really tired as the work not only began very early but also was quite physical with most of her time being on her feet; and this was after the walk of a mile to and from the bakery! Notwithstanding this, she did her best to tell her mum how much she was enjoying the world of work.

A little later, as she passed the suitcase in the hall, she noticed some papers protruding from the top pocket. She removed them and looked at the confusing diagrams. Lots of names were listed. Her mum was lying down upstairs so she took them up with her.

"What is this, Mum?"

Her mum looked dreadful and her colour had drained to match the white sheets on which she lay. Piper could only be thankful that her mum was due at the hospital to begin her treatment in two days.

Her mum sat up with some difficulty.

"Oh, let me see. My goodness, where did you get this from?"

"It was sticking out of the case downstairs. What is it?"

"Well, I can't think where it has come from. You say it came from the case?"

"Yes."

"Well, it's a family tree. You see, here are my parents and their parents and over here, a side of the family I never knew existed. Look, here you are and your dad over here. I can't think why this has appeared now and where it's come from. It shows more information than I have, certainly, and though it's nice to have I can't think that it's going to be very much use; in fact, no use at all. I think we're going to have to take that case back, Piper. It seems to be… misfiring, shall I say."

"Okay, Mum, at the weekend, I'll do as you say."

Chapter 6

Bequest

The following day, Piper was doing her best to cook a meal for herself and her mum. Piper had used up the last of her own money buying something for tea on the way home. Of even more concern than their dwindling funds, was the fact that her mum was still eating very little. The weight had dropped off her and she looked dreadful. Piper knew that the treatment was starting soon, and she knew it couldn't come soon enough.

The phone rang.

"Oh hello, is that Mary Milton?"

"No, she is having a lie down upstairs. Can I get her to phone you back?"

"Yes, we'll probably need to speak with her but might I ask who you are?"

"Yes, I'm Piper, her daughter."

"Ah, yes, very well then. I represent a firm of solicitors in Ireland, just outside Dublin. I can tell you that we have been engaged as executors of the estate of the late Kathleen Murtagh. She passed away about a month ago and our enquiries lead us to believe that your mother is the sole beneficiary of her will."

At first, Piper thought this must be a financial scam and any moment she would be expected to divulge confidential account numbers or other details. However, the more she listened, the more authentic the caller sounded. Moreover, she knew that she now had the means of looking for the late relative of her mother's simply by referring to the family tree that had just appeared from the case. Piper considered that *misfiring* was the last thing she was thinking about the case.

"Oh, how cool. I can get my mum to phone you back if you need to speak to her."

"Well, I can reveal that a significant sum of money lies in the estate, in the form of investments and also a rather large house that, though in need of some repair, has been valued for tax purposes at almost half a million euros."

"Whoa! That's a fortune! I am afraid that my mother is not very well at the moment. She is awaiting urgent treatment for leukaemia. Will it be necessary for her to travel?"

"No, by no means essential. Our business can be transacted without us seeing her in person. If we do need to see her, then I am sure there is enough equity held in the estate for us to journey to visit her. If your mother can prove who she is with a passport and a signed authority from someone who has known her for some years, like a doctor or a member of the clergy or even a local solicitor, then we can start the transfer of at least some of the funds."

Piper was now hopping up and down. Any and all doubts that she harboured about the mysterious case in the hall were swept away in an instant. She knew at that moment that the Magic Suitcase had definitely produced that family tree and she was also pretty sure that the suitcase had had a hand in the appointment that came through so quickly, her mum's blood test and, most likely, the timely change in specialist.

She took the details down on a pad and promised the solicitor that she would action her requests as soon as possible and return the information to her. She rushed upstairs to tell her mum. Mary was asleep but Piper couldn't help but wake her. She told her about the phone call and informed her that she had inherited from the estate of a relative in Ireland. Her mum was a little dazed at first but soon recognised the implications.

She reached for the family tree that was by her bed. "I must confess, I've never heard of Kathleen Murtagh, but I can see that she is here on my aunt's side of the family. It must have been a long time ago since they moved to Ireland. I don't ever remember meeting them. Did the executor inform you how much was involved?"

Piper then told her mum how much money was tied up in the estate.

Her mum shook her head as if she'd not heard her daughter. "What, and they are going to transfer it to me?!"

"Yes, Mum, subject to you proving who you are; and there is also a house, a big house in Ireland that's been bequ…bequ…

"Bequeathed," her mum offered.

"Yes, that!"

"I can't believe it. Just when my finances are pretty dreadful; just when we need it the most."

A long pause followed and Piper wondered in that moment if her mum had considered that the Magic Case had been responsible. “Well, that will certainly be a turn up for the books. How wonderful, just when the mortgage company is pushing hard, wanting me to sell the house. It should allow me to settle some debts, and hopefully, keeping a roof over our heads won’t be a problem.”

Piper just had to ask. “Mum, do you… do you think that the suitcase has anything to do with this?”

Her mum laughed. “Well, Piper, how can it have? I must confess, I was just going along with it for you. I don’t believe in magic or Magic Suitcases. I think at the weekend, we return it to the tip.”

“Oh, okay then, Mum, if you feel strongly about it.”

Although Piper would go along with her mum’s wishes, she was convinced that the Magic Suitcase was responsible for at least some of the positive things that had happened since her mum’s dreadful diagnosis. Piper was puzzled by her mother’s refusal to accept any of the mounting clues as to the wonderful things that the Magic Case had quietly carried out. However, a strong but heart-breaking clue was provided as to the priorities in her mum’s current thoughts and revealed in her next breath. “Piper, I must write a Will, just in the event something goes wrong – so you’ll be protected.”

“Mum, nothing is going to go wrong,” said the young woman with as much bravery as she could muster as she looked reassuringly back at her. By this time, her knees were trembling so much that she knew she had to leave the room.

“Oh, I was making you a cup of tea. I’ll go and get it,” became her hastily assembled excuse.

She went downstairs, catching a glimpse of her newly straightened hair in the mirror but it was the tears that filled those pretty blue eyes that consumed her as she dabbed at them furiously with a tissue that rapidly became soaked. For sure, those GHDs *were* fabulous. She patted the top of the suitcase,

“Thanks so much for my straighteners and I’m thinking of all the other things you’ve done to help.” Her voice dipped to its lowest register as she moved closer, her cheek almost touching the case, and whispered, “Please don’t let her die, I’m begging you.”

If either mother or daughter needed any more convincing as to its ability to provide help to those who were in need of it, then the Magic Suitcase moved that night to settle such things unequivocally and to remove any lingering doubts. If only it had been enough.

Chapter 7

Wonder Drug

Piper came back from her shift at the bakery in the late morning. She knew that Brett, the hospital driver, would be calling for her mum any minute now as her treatment was to begin that day.

As she came into the hallway, she noticed a box made from polystyrene on the floor. She picked up the box and opened the lid. Inside were some cool blocks and also twelve small boxes that all looked the same and which were shrink-wrapped. She saw that the boxes had unusual words on them, but she did recognise that they each had a serial number, a shiny 3D holographic security barcode and the words, 'For specialist use only'. Only then did she see that on the outside was a label with Dr Brill's name on it. She carefully replaced the lid and went to find her mum.

Brett was his usual jovial self that morning. He appeared on time, just as he always did, and patiently held the door to the car open for Mary. Piper had to help her mum from the house to the car.

On their way to the hospital, Piper told her mum about the box that she'd placed on the seat between them.

"What, you say it's got Dr Brill's name on it? Do you think he's had some treatment delivered to the house?"

Piper thought that it was about time she revealed some of her thoughts about the Magic Case. "No, Mum I think this is from the suitcase. I think this is just another in a series of helpful and kind things it has provided us with. There must be something important about it or something special." She tapped the box gently. "Let's see what Dr Brill says, shall we?"

Mary remained silent for the rest of the journey. Piper caught Brett looking in his rear-view mirror; a stare that was a little longer than safe driving would have sanctioned. In that moment, Mary looked carefully at the polystyrene box with its neat printed label featuring Dr

Brill's details and she recognised then that it bore a close resemblance to the label that had been applied to the letter addressed to her GP, which had contained the blood test forms.

Brett continued to drive and soon they were at the hospital.

Piper showed the box to Dr Brill. The look upon his face said much, which was just as well because in that moment, speech appeared to have failed him. No one could have been less prepared or more surprised by what he was about to find inside the box when he opened it. He stared at the contents, unable to take his eyes from the dozen boxes within.

Eventually, he managed words: "This is Motumixamab. It's a leading edge drug that we just cannot get hold of – because *no one* can. It's in such demand the world over and the laboratory that makes it is working flat out and still cannot meet the demand, despite their best efforts. It's perfect for your mum's condition. It's chilled as well." He pointed to the glowing blue plastic strip that indicated the temperature inside the box. "Perfect. How did you get hold of it?"

Piper was careful with her choice of words.

"It just arrived at our house, Dr Brill. We have no idea where it has come from. The box was just lying there this morning, addressed to you."

"But this is like gold dust – actually much more precious than gold! We ran through our allocation some weeks ago and can't get any more. Have you bought it? How did you find a supplier? How did you know what it was? There's almost a third of a million pounds worth in that box."

Piper gulped. Poor Dr Brill seemed agitated. All she could do was to answer his questions one-by-one as best she could. "We didn't, Dr Brill; it's the first we've heard of it. We had no idea what it was or where it came from. We couldn't afford that kind of money." Her sparkly blue eyes now had more than a hint of sadness and distress as she looked imploringly at the specialist.

One more question had occurred to him, "Do you know someone at the factory and he or she couriered it to you?"

Piper had run out of explanations and it was Mary who then spoke. "Dr Brill, it just arrived at our house and we have no idea how it got there or where it's from or who sent it. We can say no more." With this she looked at her daughter.

Dr Brill nodded, acknowledging that his shock had caused him to ask his questions more vigorously than politeness would have sanctioned. He gently squeezed their hands as he reached over the desk. The specialist then spotted something that would allow him to clarify very quickly where it had come from. He looked up at the clock on the wall.

"Oh look, there are batch numbers here on each box. Could you excuse me? I'm going to try and catch the manufacturers in Japan."

He left the room looking really troubled. Mary and Piper stared at each other a little sheepishly while he was gone but they realised they could or should not say any more. He returned a few minutes later.

"This batch is scheduled for production this coming week! You seem to have, somehow, taken delivery early!

There then came a lengthy pause. Dr Brill was clearly stunned by what had taken place and wasn't really sure what to say next. He stared at the box. At this point, he looked as if he needed to go and lie down but he remembered at that moment the poor state and needs of his patient.

Suddenly, he pulled himself up to his full height. He realised that neither patient nor daughter could possibly give him any more information. His only course of action now was not to overthink it and simply take what was on offer. He had a life to save.

"Anyway…" – he thought was a good word to use to reset his thoughts – "this is just what we need. It's just what *you* need." He suggested as he looked eagerly at his patient. "This is the finest treatment we've ever seen for your condition and there is enough here to treat you, and several others." He tapped the box as he spoke.

Within moments, the specialist had set up a drip with the Motumixamab running through it. Dr Brill glanced encouragingly at patient, daughter and his nurse assistant. He was confident this would give his patient the very best chance of success.

And sure enough, Dr Brill's optimism was borne out by events. Brett continued to collect Mary and her daughter for each and every appointment. The drips went up and the treatment continued. Mary suffered very few side effects and within a week or two, she began to feel a lot better.

Then, after a few weeks, things turned nasty. Mary, after showing some initial improvement, suddenly became very weak and very tired. Piper thought with some alarm, when she looked at her mum, that she looked like a ghost. At her next appointment, Dr Brill took her blood tests, sent them for urgent analysis and was devastated to the point of disbelief by what came back. He looked at the printout of the blood results. He looked again, unable to speak. No sentence of death could ever have been clearer. The wonder drug had failed. Mary's blood cancer had countered, in its stride, the finest treatment known to man – the very best that specialists had ever seen – and in its place, it had left a patient who would be lucky to see the end of the month without an absolute miracle occurring. He realised, ruefully, that the miracle had just failed.

In truth, his expression said much, and Mary and Piper knew something of the words they were about to hear.

Before he spoke, he glanced at his nurse and almost imperceptibly shook his head. Both Mary and Piper gulped while Zoe looked away quickly, quite unable to meet Mary's glance at her.

"Mary I'm sorry, the leukaemia, after an initial response, has come back with a vengeance. We are going to have to keep you in hospital and organise some more blood transfusions for you. Our only course of action now is to…to…continue your treatment…and to do a marrow transplant." He struggled with his words, his disappointment so deep. "This depends on whether we can find a donor. I am so sorry about this. I'll phone the ward and get a bed for you. Once I have done this I'll answer all your questions."

He and Zoe left the room, leaving Mary and Piper on their own. Piper was a brave girl. There weren't many scenarios that she hadn't thought through in her mind and yet she had seen what the Magic Suitcase could do and when the special treatment had appeared, she'd thought that would only be a matter of time until her mum was safe. She did her best to control the tears that were gathering steadily in the corners of her eyes, doing her utmost to be brave for the sake of her mum. For the first time ever, she realised that she was contemplating a life on her own.

Mary spoke first, "Don't you worry about me. I'll get through this. It looks as though this magic drug has failed. It looks as though your Magic Suitcase has failed." She smiled a weak smile that barely disguised what lay within. "Will you be all right on your own? Uh…I mean at home…while I am in hospital. You may need to think about phoning your dad, Piper."

"Oh, don't worry about me, Mum. I will ask Brett if he will bring me back each day to visit you, and Mrs Stevens next door will look out for me." The tears that continued to build now stung her mercilessly as she attempted her next words. "I can't speak to dad. He has not answered any of your texts has he, Mum? Where is he, Mum? He has not been interested, not in you nor in me; not since he met, 'the love of his life and soul mate'!".

"Try not to blame him, Piper, you know men do stupid things sometimes."

Piper smiled, she knew that her mum had done her best not to call him but her own fleeting smile only framed the tears that were still building relentlessly and then became a flood.

Piper did her best to stem their flow with a tissue that from the outset was not equal to the task, but by thinking about her mum and what she needed at that moment, she restored some of her calm. Having her mum worry about her was most definitely not going to help.

"I'll be here each day, Mum. I promise, whatever happens. You are right, Mum, it looks like the Magic Suitcase has let us down."

"Ah well, look it was worth a go and as you heard, Dr Brill has plenty of other ideas yet. I'm sure he will find a donor. Once he has done this, he'll have me home in no time. Are you going to be okay for money, Piper?"

"Yes. Work have paid my wages, so you are now looking at a wealthy woman! And I hear that you are about to come into a shed load of money too, so we'll be okay. For once, that's the least of our worries, eh?" she said, as she did her best to generate a smile through the tears that continued to inundate her pretty blue eyes, which were now swollen and sore.

"It's late, my darling, you get off and I'll get up to the ward. I haven't told you how much I love you and what a wonderful daughter you are. I am so sorry I haven't said that to you each minute of every day." Such words had the effect off restarting the tears that Piper was desperately trying to control. More than this, she realised that her mum was acknowledging just how poorly she knew herself to be.

The nurse brought in some bags of blood and a transfusion began at once.

Piper hugged her mum and kissed her, "I love you, too, Mum. Don't worry about me, I'll be fine on my own at home and I'll see you tomorrow." She asked nurse Zoe if she could do the tissue type test on her to see if she'd be a suitable donor for her mum. Zoe said that she'd do it as soon as she'd taken Mary up to the ward and send it urgently.

The nurse put Mary in a chair in order to wheel her to the ward. Piper left the outpatient department after having her cheek swab for tissue typing. She pulled out her phone to see if she could get a taxi but to her surprise, Brett was waiting there.

"Oh, Miss Piper, so nice to see you. I was just dropping off another patient."

He looked with concern at her tear stained face.

"Would you like a lift home, Miss?"

"Is that okay? You won't get in trouble, will you? And it seems really late for you to still be working."

"Oh, Miss. don't you worry about that. They pay me really well, so I try to do a few extra journeys to make up for their kindness to me and especially so since my wife died. You jump in and I will have you home in a jiffy."

Brett could tell by the look on Piper's face that things had gone badly. Notwithstanding this, she told him how sorry she was to hear about his wife.

They soon reached home.

"Brett, I have an errand to run. Could I impose on you a bit longer? I won't be a minute, I promise."

"Oh yes of course, Miss."

Piper ran into the house. She grabbed the case from the hallway.

"Would it be okay for you to take me to the local tip, please? It won't take a minute, and I can walk back from there."

Brett parked his car at the tip. He helped Piper get the case from the boot.

"Can I help you, Miss?"

"No, Brett, thank you. You have been so kind. This is something I have to do on my own."

He remained by the car as she walked away from him, pulling the case behind her. The wheels made more of a clatter than usual and the golden zips now took on the appearance of rust that seemed only to be complemented by the grey clouds and the drizzle that began in that moment. The girl and the case made for a distressing scene as they moved slowly towards the tip.

This was it. She was quite alone. Moreover, she realised then that this situation would always apply from this moment on. She paused as if catching a glimpse of the sad and lonely future that awaited her. The rain became heavier; there was now nothing and no one to bear witness to the salty tears that stung her cheeks even more than the cold rain that enveloped her as she stood there.

She walked toward the edge of the skip marked ‘General Waste’.

The rain became heavier and heavier just as Piper’s tears became sobs of despair that she no longer had the strength to control. The rain drenched her but it was the tears that filled her eyes, flowed down her cheeks and became unstoppable.

The old man looked at the heart-breaking scene, unable to move. He was soon drenched too and he could only hope that the rain might hide his own tears as he stood watching Piper on her lonely walk.

Piper lifted the case up so that she could throw it over the guard rail that ran next to the skip but as she did so, she felt the case become heavier. Something was inside.

She brought the case down and felt inside the pocket. She withdrew a pink and blue toy unicorn head in a soft, fluffy material. It shone, or so it appeared, despite the dull day and the rain.

She paused for a minute or so, just staring at the soft toy, stroking it gently.

“Is everything all right, Miss?” the old man called, his voice cracking. He swiped with a thickened palm at his tears, desperately trying to restore his composure.

Piper pulled the case away from the skip and clung to the unicorn as she returned to the car.

“Please Brett, could you take us home?”

“That I will, Miss. May I ask, what is that?” he asked, nodding at the soft toy.

“It’s a promise. A promise that was made to me many years ago but never kept.”

Brett could ask no more and silence descended on the car as he drove Piper home and helped her, once again, remove the case from the boot.

“Are you going to be all right, Miss? Is there anyone we need to call?”

“No Brett, thank you but there is no one *to* call.”

She made for the front door. Her next-door neighbour, Mrs Stevens, had seen her approach and rushed out of her house. Brett nodded to her from where he stood beside his car.

"I'll be back for you tomorrow, Miss, so you can visit your mum."

The strange thing was, Piper didn't remember telling Brett about her mum. He must have seen this a hundred times before.

Mrs Stevens had seen that Piper was on her own and had also feared the worse. "You get yourself settled and I'll be right over with some tea for you, my girl. We have to keep your strength up. Maybe change out of those wet clothes or you'll catch your death." She coughed suddenly, fearing that she had said the wrong thing.

Brett did his best to smile at the neighbour who seemed like a kind elderly lady, but still felt very sad. He turned to get back in the car.

Piper placed the soaking wet case back in the hallway. She stroked the unicorn with the lovely soft fur. She remembered her own birthday now some years ago when her father had asked her what she wanted as a present. She'd seen the most beautiful toy unicorn; it was just like the one she held. At that time, it was widely available and very popular. She asked her dad if he would get one for her. He promised that he would.

A couple of weeks later, on her birthday, he told her that he'd been too busy to find one and simply gave her an envelope with some money inside. She was six years old. Demand had been so high that her mum had subsequently been unable to find one in the shops.

Now it seemed that the promise, made ten years ago, had been kept by someone or something else. Perhaps it was a moment to pause; perhaps it was a promise that she wasn't on her own and must not lose hope despite the dreadful news and the desolate mood that ran through her.

Mrs Stevens soon returned with a magnificent bowl of hot stew. She sat with Piper, making sure that she at least made a start on the nourishing meal. She also did her best to make polite conversation and tried not to ask difficult questions. In truth, Piper's return alone had alerted her to the fact that news was not good. She reflected on her friend who had died from a similar diagnosis and gave an involuntary shiver as she sat with Piper.

The following day, Piper telephoned the bakery early to say that she would have to give up her job. They were very kind and promised to transfer the rest of her wages that day. They also said that she could return any time should her mum's condition improve, something that they all earnestly hoped for.

Then Brett appeared and whisked her away to see her mother.

She sat by the hospital bed but her mum was very tired and spent most of the time asleep. The drips and pumps whirred quietly, and Piper could see that they were still giving her blood. She looked paler than the nurses' pristine white uniforms and Dr Brill's white coat.

Dr Brill came over to her and spoke quietly even though he'd taken her to his office and closed the door.

"I'm sorry Piper. Things are really serious. We've checked all the databases for a suitable donor for your mum, but none came close, not nearly close enough. Of course, we can go with the nearest match, but I am not hopeful."

Piper looked at Dr Brill. She was not surprised: she'd had an uneasy feeling yesterday just witnessing the way he'd glanced at his specialist nurse.

"Zoe has sent off your test to see if you are a match for your mum. It should be back very soon. I'll let you know straight away if you are. Why not get home and get some rest? We will phone you at once if there's any change?"

Piper went on to the high dependency unit where they'd moved her mum. The blood transfusion was still running. No doubt this was the only thing keeping her alive at that moment. She kissed her mum and squeezed her hand.

She went out to the taxi rank to see if she could get a taxi home, but Brett was there again.

"My goodness, what a coincidence. I wondered if that was you. Are you going home, Miss Piper?"

"Yes please, Brett. You always seem to be here, just when I need you. You must work some long hours."

"Oh, that I do, Miss Piper."

On the journey home, Brett did his best to make made polite conversation and could only repeat that he hoped her mum was going to be all right.

When Piper got home, she saw that a leaflet had been pushed through the door. It was for a blood drive at the local health clinic. They were starting that day and they'd be there for two days. She saw how much blood they'd given her mum and decided there and then to become a donor.

Chapter 8

The Match

The next day, Piper walked up the road to the local health clinic to see if they were up and running. She took a new registration form from the table and filled it in with her details. Dr Brill had phoned her first thing to inform her that her tissue typing test showed that she was not a good match for her mother.

The 'enquiries' window was busy, so Piper sat down after putting her form in the tray provided. They'd clearly had a good response to the local leaflet drop as the chairs in generously proportioned waiting room were steadily occupied.

A little while later, a young, tall man arrived and went to speak to the staff at the window. The receptionist looked at the donor's registration card.

"Oh, Mr Brogan, I don't know why they've cancelled your appointment at the blood bank and sent you all the way over here. We are based there and the clinic should be running as normal. They should have been able to take your sample at once rather than sending you out of your way. I am so sorry."

The young man smiled, shrugged his shoulders a little but otherwise was not perturbed. "No matter, as long as I can donate here, then it's no problem. My dad drove me over and he said he didn't mind the drive. He even said he'd wait for me in the car, so it's all good."

She smiled back at the handsome man, her heart skipping along as she spoke. "Thanks for being so understanding. If you'd please take a seat, we should be starting soon."

He moved to occupy one of the few remaining free seats next to a balding old man. A large Alsatian sat next to him panting slowly in the warm room. The dog looked up at the young man as he came over. He couldn't occupy the seat as the dog was in the way.

"Please excuse my dog, he is a comfort dog. I am so anxious I can't go anywhere without him. I'm afraid, when he's sat next to me like this, there's simply no moving him."

"Oh, don't worry it's no problem. Please don't move him, there are other seats. I can sit elsewhere," replied the young man.

"Sorry about that," the old man chuckled as much to himself as to the young man and the dog.

The young man patted the dog and stroked him behind his ears. The Alsatian looked back at him, as a large floppy pink tongue appeared and somehow managed to lick the end of his long nose.

"Oh, he likes, you."

The young chap smiled again and moved to another empty chair just around the corner. He sat next to Piper.

"Hi, I'm Colin." He saw how nervous she looked. "Is this your first time?"

"Yes, how can you tell? I always look like this especially just before I faint and hit the floor."

He laughed, "Oh don't worry I'll get ready to catch you."

She offered a depleted smile in return. "My mum is having so much blood at St Catherine's, I thought I'd better show up and become a donor."

"Oh, St Catherine's, they have the specialist blood unit there, don't they? Is she poorly?"

"Yes, she has a nasty blood disorder."

Colin swallowed hard and went very pale. A pause opened up as he stared at the floor, breaking eye contact.

"Oh, I am so sorry to hear that, I hope she gets better."

"Are you a regular? I saw that you have one of those little red books they give you. Sorry for being so nosey."

He laughed. "Just observant, I'm sure. And yes, for a little while – as soon as I was old enough."

"Oh wow! That's really good of you. What made you join up?"

"Well… I just fancied it and thought it was the right thing to do, I guess."

"Piper Milton," called out the receptionist.

"Excuse me, that's me. Wish me luck."

The young man smiled engagingly and Piper went to the desk.

"I'm sorry, Miss Milton, but you are only sixteen. We have a policy of eighteen and over, seventeen as an absolute minimum, so I am afraid you are not eligible to donate. Thank you for coming and as soon as you reach eighteen, you'll be welcome here, of course"

She went back to speak to Colin, "Oh, seems as though I am not wanted. Lucky reprieve, I guess; although, I was keen to do my bit."

"Yes, they were a bit reluctant to take mine twelve months ago I was still 17. It was only…only when I'd impressed upon them how important it was."

"I'll come back when I'm a bit older. So, for now, it seems they don't want my blood and Dr Brill, the specialist, says that I am not a good match for my mum."

"Oh I see. So she's *really* poorly then? I am so sorry."

Piper smiled, thanked Colin for his kindness and interest and walked through the exit.

A little while later, Colin had donated a pint of blood and was leaving the clinic when the old gentleman with the dog stopped him in the corridor.

"Do you drive young man?" he asked with a chuckle.

"No, no Sir, at least not yet. I have my test coming up."

"Oh my, well when you take it, good luck. In fact, I have a lucky keyring here. Would you like it?"

The old chap handed the keyring over before Colin could speak. He then looked at the dog who had not taken his eyes off him. "Come on then, boy, we'd better get home." The Alsatian looked once more at his master and started walking to the exit.

"Good luck with your test tomorrow, young man."

Colin thought the old man could only have guessed that his test was the next day, although he had been careful not to reveal exactly when. The fewer people who knew when his test was, the fewer he'd have to tell if he should fail. He found his dad in the car park.

"All done, Colin?"

"Oh yes Dad, thanks for bringing me out this way."

"Did they say why your appointment at your usual clinic had been cancelled?"

"No, they couldn't understand it. They say it's open and working as normal. Funny thing."

"Dad, did you see a young girl walk out? Pretty girl with long hair."

"Yes, now that you mention it. Why?"

"She wanted to donate but she's just sixteen and, like they did with me a couple of years ago, they told her she is too young." A slight pause opened before Colin continued. "Dad, her mum has leukaemia, like Mum."

Colin's dad nodded; he knew which words would come next.

"I want to get tested, Dad. I was too young to help Mum. Can I have the test, Dad?"

Colin's dad, Jeffrey, looked at his son. It had been many years since his wife had died of an aggressive leukaemia. He knew that it still haunted his young son, just as it did him, even though it was now so long ago.

Words failed in that instance and Jeffrey simply nodded as he lived, once more, those painful memories that time had barely dulled.

"She's under Dr Brill, Dad, like Mum was. "

"Okay," Jeffrey said simply and nodded again. "So, do you want me to speak to Dr Brill?"

"I bet he'll be there now, Dad. It's just a cheek swab."

"What are you thinking? Is it about that poor girl? You know the chances of you being a match, and a good match, are slim? Perhaps very slim I should say – even vanishingly…."

"Yes, yes, I know that, Dad, but at least I'll have tried. If they put my results in their database, I may be able to help someone, somewhere – even if it's *not* her. Maybe, if someone had tried for Mum?"

Jeffrey nodded; these were his thoughts exactly. "I know, I know. It was a long time ago but I remember." Jeffrey pressed the start button and the car engine sprang to life – the decision was made, "Let's go and see if his nurse is around, shall we?"

Jeffrey drove to St Catherine's. He knew just where to go and the person he needed to speak with. He had spent so many days, nights and weekends in the ward, hoping and praying that his wife would get better. It was not to be. Dr Brill was not there, but Zoe phoned him while the two men waited, and he asked her if she'd do the test as requested.

The following day, Colin sat with his instructor at the test centre. He had a new car, one that Colin had not driven before. He went through the controls as quickly as he could because time was limited. They'd been a bit late getting to the test centre. The examiner was impatient to begin the test.

All went well and the examiner marked Colin's score off on his test sheet. It then started to rain and Colin's mind went blank. He looked at the windscreen, which was rapidly being covered by the raindrops.

"Please put on the windscreen wipers," the examiner instructed.

Colin couldn't remember about the control of the windscreen wipers. The examiner sensed his dilemma. He knew this was an important component of the test.

"I am sorry, but if I have to activate the wipers for you then there will be no alternative for me but to fail you."

Colin started to panic; he looked across the steering column and the dash. The more he saw, the less he recognised. He then noticed the keyring that the old man had given him in the clinic. He could only think to himself what a fat lot of good it had done for him. He knew he was a second away from failing, perhaps less.

Suddenly, he must have touched something, although he would always wonder if this was the case. The wipers came on with a quick and powerful sweep that cleared the windscreen immediately and continued to do so. The examiner nodded and looked back at his clipboard. They arrived back at the test centre and the examiner informed Colin that he'd passed. Colin thanked him and shook his hand.

"A bit of a close call for a moment, Mr Brogan, but I am satisfied that you have met the requirements." Colin went to find his instructor who drove him home. Colin rubbed the keyring. They pulled up at the large house that was set back from the road. The instructor nodded to the small red car on the drive.

"Is that your little car?" asked the instructor.

"Yes, Dad bought it for me, he said he didn't doubt that I'd pass. It was a close thing, though."

"Yes, I'm so sorry about the wipers. I should have gone through things in more detail. Still, you managed to get them to come on. Well done, otherwise it would have been a clear fail. The examiner didn't have a choice."

Colin rubbed the key ring in his pocket again and smiled.

By this time, Piper was spending every day at the hospital. Brett came for her each morning and somehow, he was always available when she needed to go home. Her neighbours were exceptional and all rallied round to call on her, to feed her and to make sure that she was coping. Sadly, each visit to her mum showed a further deterioration. Her fear was that one day she would turn up and the bed would be empty.

Some days later, however, Dr Brill greeted her almost as soon as she stepped out of the car. If Piper hadn't known better, she could have sworn he was about to do a little dance or at least had been waiting for her to arrive. He grabbed both her hands and almost lifted her off the floor.

"Piper, we have a match! Not just any match but a fabulous match. In fact, in all my years in medicine, I have rarely seen a match like this." He became more serious; there was something he needed to ask her. "Look, this is a bit unconventional, but the donor says he is ready to go as soon as we are. Time is pressing, we want to get it done today. He says, if you and your mum are willing, that he'd very much like to meet you. I have to say that this is entirely up to you. We totally respect patient confidentiality. Treatment will still go ahead, even if you say no. Your mum is happy with this and says it's your call."

"Then if it's okay, I'd also like to meet him. I'd like to thank him."

The specialist nodded, "Very well then; I thought you'd say that, he's in the next room."

Piper was shown into the adjoining room. The young man in there was all gowned up ready for the marrow donation.

"You!"

"Me!"

"Oh my! It's Colin isn't it? Thank you, thank you so much for doing this for my mum and for me." Tears filled her eyes. She had to switch the topic of conversation quickly to divert her thoughts. "I hope it's not going to be painful!"

"Oh, if you hear me scream then run in or you could even stay and hold my hand!"

"Oh no, not me, I faint just at the sight of needles. Did you not see how pale I was at that clinic last week?"

"Actually, I thought pale and interesting."

With this, however, Piper sat next to Colin and gripped his hand. "It's the least I can do," she offered brightly, "I guess I might as well stay with you as they tell me mum is now in isolation."

"Oh Piper, this is my dad." Jeffrey stood up and shook Piper's hand.

"Pleased to meet you, Sir. I'm Piper."

"Oh, yes, Piper, I can say I've heard *all* about you."

"Dad!"

"From Dr Brill, of course," he recovered quickly, sparing his son embarrassment. "Please call me Jeffrey, Piper. Colin is so pleased to be able to help you. It was such an unusual thing his bumping into you in the way he did. I don't know what the chances are that he should prove to be such a perfect and compatible donor for your mum. He's always wanted to do something like this, ever since…"

"Dad!" interrupted Colin. "Dad, they are going to start."

Jeffrey looked at his son. He knew that he didn't want to burden the young girl with their secrets and their past.

"Well, in that case, I think I am going to get myself a coffee and a sticky bun from the nice café they have here. Are you sure you don't want to come with me, Piper? He can be a big baby, you know. It might not be very pretty."

"Dad! Thanks for the vote of confidence."

"Just saying, son. He used to scream having a plaster put on his knee when he fell off his bike. I think you'll need earplugs to protect your hearing."

"Dad," I think they're about to sell the last sticky bun, so I'd hurry if I were you."

"Now he's trying to get rid of me."

Dr Brill laughed. "We need to insert the trochar about here. He pointed to the front of Colin's hip. This is the least painful area and usually gives us the best sample. Anyone feeling like running out?" he said, looking at Piper.

"Last chance, Piper," Jeffrey said.

Piper was holding Colin's hand now with both of hers. "He's holding on so tight, I don't think I can move. Besides they'll need help picking you up, Colin, if you faint."

"Right, I'll see you two later. Will I be able to hear the screams from the café?"

"Oh no, don't worry, I can't feel a thing." Piper said as Jeffrey laughed and left the room.

Colin laughed. "I reckon you'll owe me a burger after all this."

"Yes, and if you don't scream too much, I'll even throw in a milkshake."

"Deal!" Colin screwed his eyes closed as the trochar went in, but only for a second. He found, as he opened his eyes, Piper was staring at him while she squeezed his hand without pause.

Once again, Dr Brill was as good as his name. The procedure was completed in no time and Colin was pleasantly surprised that it was nowhere as bad as he'd anticipated. He clung to Piper's hand perhaps a little harder than he would have wished but he noticed, it seemed for the first time, those gorgeous blue eyes that were hinted at under the fringe of slightly unruly blonde hair. She smiled once more, just before she let go and he heard her say very quietly.

"Thank you, ever so much. You are a life saver."

"My pleasure," he whispered back, "I hope I am; and you did say milkshake as well, didn't you?"

"Oh, that's my promise. I could even go for a large one. I'd better let you get dressed."

Colin looked down at his knees peeping from under the gown.

"Don't start blushing now, just because you've seen my knobbly knees!"

"Not bad those legs; nicer than mine."

"Oh, you poor soul. Still nice smile!"

"Thank you," she said, as she blushed uncontrollably.

Nurse Zoe smiled and Dr Brill winked back at her.

"Right, we're going to gown up and get to your mum, Piper. You won't be able to see her yet as we need to keep her in isolation. Her own immune system has been destroyed, as, hopefully, has the blood cancer and if the new marrow takes, then it will need some time. We'll need your mum to stay with us for at least thirty days. You can visit as often as you like but your mum will be in isolation to protect her."

Piper nodded. "That's fine. I just hope that you've succeeded."

"I promise this is her best chance."

"I know. Thank you, Dr Brill and thank you, Colin.

"I'll do anything for a burger and milkshake."

She smiled a glorious smile that caused Colin to blush and his heart to flutter.

"Is there anyone at home with you, Piper? Your mum told me about your dad." The specialist looked away as embarrassment intruded.

Piper nodded, acknowledging his sensitivity towards her. “That’s okay, Dr Brill. No, there’s no one at home but my neighbours are very kind and have been looking in on me. One of them even cut my fringe!”

“And you are sixteen, Piper?”

“Yes.”

“We can involve social services and or the cancer charities if you need any help,” confirmed Dr Brill.

“Oh no, I’m fine, Dr Brill, thank you.”

Jeffrey returned, Piper nodded to Colin, “I nearly fainted but he was really brave,” she admitted.

“Well that’s a first. No doubt he had to be brave with you sitting next to him, Piper.”

“Dad, Piper is all alone.” Colin began. “Can she come home with us?”

“Yes, if she wishes. Would you like that, Piper? We have a very nice spare room with an en-suite. In fact lots of spare rooms! There’s just me and Colin in the house and you’ll have your own space.”

Piper thought for a minute and she glanced at Colin. In that moment her answer appeared.

“That would be very kind. Are you sure I won’t be any trouble?”

“No, not at all, we are rattling round in that big house ever since ever since…well, for a while, shall I say. Well, it’s all settled,” Jeffrey concluded.

“Dad’s a great cook, Piper, though I could do with someone helping out with all that veg he shovels down me.”

Piper laughed, “Well, it doesn’t look as if it’s done you any harm.”

Nurse Zoe spoke, “Colin, we’ll keep you for an hour or two but then you are free to be discharged. Your GP can perform some check bloods in a few days to make sure you are not anaemic; otherwise as regards your mum, Piper, it’s now a waiting game.”

“Can I see her, Zoe?”

“No, I’m afraid it’s a bit soon. But tomorrow, quite possibly.”

A couple of hours later, Piper left the hospital with Jeffrey and Colin. She looked to see if Brett was there but for the first time, he must have been out collecting other patients.

Chapter 9

Refuge

Jeffrey and Colin took Piper back to her home to pick up a few things. She did some packing, placing her things and her GHDs in what she now absolutely knew was a Magic Suitcase. She knelt by the side of it as she whispered. "Thank You."

Colin and his Dad waited in the car.

Piper spoke to one or two of her neighbours who had become used to rushing out of their houses as soon as she appeared. She told them she would be spending some time with friends. Colin and his Dad came out of the car at this point and Mrs Stevens nodded approvingly to Piper as she looked at Colin. Jeffrey passed a sheet of paper with their address and telephone number just in case they needed to contact Piper.

Colin put the case in the boot. "Oh, what a magnificent old case."

Piper smiled. She wondered if he could ever realise just how magnificent. Jeffrey drove them home. His car pulled on to the long drive. Piper looked at the grand old house that had been beautifully restored.

"Whoa! How beautiful. What a big house!"

"It's too big for us now, Piper, but feel free to call it home for as long as you need. I was thinking, we have lots of room, if she wishes, your mum can come here for a convalescence. You can ask her when the time is right." Jeffrey suggested.

Colin showed her up to her room. It had beautiful curtains pinned back, framing the large bay window, with inset wooden panelling, that looked out onto the extensive grounds.

"Oh, how cool is that! It's like a hotel!" Piper rushed over to the window.

"Well, you can stay as long as you want and you'll have your own space so don't feel you have to come and socialise if you want to be on your own." Piper nodded as Colin placed the case on the bed. "I'll leave you to unpack," he went on, "As I said, Dad is a super cook so if you want to wander down when you are ready, we'll feed you."

Later that evening, Jeffrey was in his study having left the two younger ones in the sitting room. The TV was on but they were talking.

"Thank you so much, having me to stay. It's so good of you. Your dad is lovely and so kind."

"Shh, don't tell him, but he loves having someone else to fuss over, not just me. Listen, don't give it another thought – no seriously, I was just pleased to be able to help."

She wanted to ask about something that she knew had been hinted at but remained unsaid.

"May I ask, you and your dad? I hope I'm not prying, am I?"

"No, not at all. I didn't want to worry you. Yes, my mum died when I was young."

"I'm so sorry."

"We are okay; of course, we both still miss her," he nodded towards the study door. "That's why I had to help. My mum died of a similar blood disorder to your mum. There was no match, not for her; nothing could be done. As I said, it was some years ago. I just knew that I wanted to help someone. I asked my dad if I could be tissue typed as soon as I met you and heard about your mum. Of course, I couldn't know it was your mum I'd be helping! I'm just so pleased that my appointment was cancelled that day and they diverted me to the same clinic you attended. Funny thing though, when I phoned to ask them, they said the clinic was open as normal and they didn't understand why I had been diverted, or by whom, across town."

Piper nodded but said nothing. She knew exactly how this had come about. No doubt this was another burst of magic that the red suitcase had managed – somehow!

The following day, Piper visited her mum. She remained in isolation, but Piper was able to look through the window and speak to her via intercom. Her mum still looked dreadful and remained very tired. She left with promises to return the following day.

Colin waited for her, saying that she was about to take her life in her own hands for the second time that day as he had just passed his test.

"Funny, I was all set to fail and then I looked at this key ring that the elderly gentleman gave me."

"Did you know him? Have you seen him before? What was his name?

"Oh, I couldn't say. I've never seen him before. He did have a big dog with him, which was funny, as the clinic says dogs are not allowed. Even more weird is that when I made enquiries, nobody could remember seeing him. I thought it was a bit odd his wanting to give me a keyring then wishing me luck for the next day, especially since I had avoided telling anyone when my test was."

Piper smiled and nodded, "Well, he was correct! It acted as a good luck charm for you."

"Yes indeed! It's a bit of an unusual thing to offer, I guess, but he seemed like a friendly old chap and I didn't want to refuse. I don't know if it brought me luck or not but anyway, I passed."

"I am sure it brought you luck and I'm so pleased you passed."

"He was in the clinic, Piper, with that big dog. Did you see him?"

"No, I can't say I did. The only person I remember was you…when you came to sit next to me. And how glad I am that you did."

"Anyway, look, I told Dad that we are going out for a burger tonight. Is that okay? You aren't too tired? I know it must be very hard on you at the moment."

"No, that would be really nice. It's on me, remember?"

"You know, I was only joking."

"I think I had the best of it – save a life in exchange for a burger."

"And a milkshake." He reminded her.

"Just how could I refuse? Still sounds like a bargain."

She smiled and looked at him. She paused, not quite sure what to say next. Her pretty eyes locked on his as she did so and as their eyes met, he felt his pulse kick in with some force while his breathing picked up; he looked away, quickly. He knew that pauses in the conversation combined with eye content could reveal much and that perhaps it was more than she should be burdened with just at that time.

That afternoon, Piper sat in the large orangery at the back of the house that looked out over the gardens. She tried to catch up on some reading but her thoughts were miles away.

Colin came in a little while later and hesitated at the entrance.

"I'm not disturbing you, am I?"

She smiled, by way of reply. Her smile, one that swept in like clear mountain air banishing the city smog, like oxygen itself. It was a smile he found himself needing more and more.

“My dad says I need to give you some space.”

“Don’t be silly. I couldn’t really get into this book and I’ve been on my own for so long with my mum being ill. My dad had walked out and though she didn’t let on, I knew he hadn’t returned any of her texts and calls. She was spending her days in bed or on the sofa as she was so tired. I had no one to talk to and then, of course, I bumped into you at the blood clinic – just before I was about to faint.”

“Yes, I remember being just like that on my first visit.”

“It’s so nice to have someone to talk to, and to be truthful, I’m glad of the company.”

A little while later Jeffrey came out of his study but stood just out of sight. He picked up on the animated chatter and the laughter both from their guest and his son. It had been years since he’d heard such things. He smiled and gently slipped back to his study, closing the door carefully.

After a couple of hours, Colin said he was going to take a quick shower and get ready for their burger night. Piper thought she’d do the same.

She went into her room and ran the shower. She picked out her best jeans and favourite t-shirt. She noticed that the suitcase had fallen over and was on its side. She picked it up and spotted that there was something inside. She could see the pale blue fabric and slowly withdrew a pretty dress, which was just in her size, and also some navy shoes. The colours seemed to complement her perfectly and although it was only a burger bar, she couldn’t wait to shower and try them on. She quickly straightened her hair and went down the wide stairs that led to the hall, to find Colin waiting for her.

She was sure that he gasped and held his breath in that moment.

The lovely dress with the flared skirt and gathered waist with the slim gold belt looked fabulous; she’d never owned anything quite so pretty.

“Wow! Piper, you look amazing.”

“Thank you, Colin, and I just love your jacket.” He glanced away as nervousness intruded but just had to look again as she stood next to him.

He nodded to her slim legs. “I thought you said you had knobbly knees like mine?”

She went with his tease, “Oh, not quite as long perhaps but surely just as knobbly.”

“No Piper, can’t see that. You look wonderful.”

Jeffrey appeared. “Are you two off then?” He too, stopped open-mouthed as he looked at Piper. His wife had always wanted a daughter. He glanced at his son who seemed, in that moment, to be oblivious to everything apart from their guest, and he smiled as he nodded to himself.

“Okay then, have fun you two and enjoy your burgers.”

“Thanks, Dad, we’ll see you later?”

“Well, I’m hoping to catch an early night,” he lied – he’d not had a decent night’s sleep since his wife had passed away – “so feel free to get back as late as you like. Just have a good time.” He watched as they went through the door. How pleased his wife would have been to see their son in the company of such a delightful and pretty girl.

Colin and Piper arrived at the burger bar. He held the door open for her. As Piper walked in, heads turned: boys stared at her and other young women stared, too, as they followed the boys’ line of sight.

“I thought I’d be over dressed but it’s quite a posh burger place,” she said, as she looked around the room.

“Yes, and everyone is looking at that pretty girl, I think,” he replied, as his eyes fixed on her.

“Not that handsome guy?” She nodded back at Colin on the other side of the table who blushed and broke eye contact quickly.

“Oh no, I guess they’re all envious of me being in your company,” he suggested. She smiled the smile that he found himself longing more and more for. “What can I get you, then?” he asked.

“Oh no! No you don’t, it’s on me, remember.”

She went to the counter and ordered the burgers and drinks and returned to the table. More eyes followed her as she moved across the room.

“It’s so kind of you and your dad to put me up or, perhaps, put up with me would be better. You know too that I’m so…”

“Oh no, don’t you dare. We’ve been through this. I didn’t know it would be your mum; *your* mum that I was able to help. I did know, if they were able to find a match, that it would be *someone*; someone with a life that was worth saving. I'm pleased I did it for you though, as otherwise, I might never have got to know you but I very badly wanted to help a poorly patient – somewhere."

"I know, and I'll never be able to thank you enough."

"Please don't think you owe me anything. Or at least," he nodded to his burger and milkshake, "consider it paid in full."

She smiled and she laughed, but the moment was fleeting as an instant later, she reached across the table, grabbed his hand gently, and suddenly became more serious. "No, thank you; I mean it."

"I know, I know, but consider this. This is not just for your mum but my mum too. She'd be very pleased, in fact, absolutely delighted."

He looked up and met her gaze just as she continued to look intently at him. He recognised that moment as it arose, he'd been nervous, frightened and trying to avoid it, thinking it couldn't possibly be the case; and yet here it was. Later, when she was alone and drifting off to sleep, she would recognise it, too.

Some time later, they left the burger bar and walked around the small town looking into shop windows and chatting. Piper was a little unsteady in the unaccustomed shoes so Colin offered her a hand and then an arm as they walked and walked through the quiet streets. She felt comfortable and relaxed just by being with him. They arrived home a little later.

The following day, Piper went in to see her mum. Colin offered to drive her and accepted without hesitation when she asked him if he wanted to go in with her. Dr Brill was waiting for her.

"Good news Piper, it looks as if you mum's blood is recovering. It's still early days but this is exactly what we want to see." Overcome by emotion, she hugged, Zoe, Colin who blushed and then could not resist hugging Dr Brill.

She looked at both men and Zoe. "Thank you so much. Can I see her?"

"Yes, I think we can make that happen. You'll have to gown up as your mum's immune system is still regenerating, but otherwise, it should be fine. You won't be able to stay in there too long."

"Oh, that's cool, as long as I'm allowed, and I'll come straight out again."

Mary was sitting up in bed. There was still an infusion of blood running and other drips, but she looked so much better despite still being very pale.

"Mum, I am so pleased to see you. They say I can't kiss you but here's a virtual one," as she smacked her lips under the tight-fitting mask.

"Oh Piper, I am feeling so much better and that kind boy, Colin was it?"

"Yes Mum, and he's right outside. I'm not quite sure where he came from, but they say he's as good a match for you as they are ever going to see. He's so nice and his dad's really cool too. I hope you don't mind, but I've ben staying with him and his dad. His mum died some years ago. They are lovely people and they say you'll be welcome there too when you are ready to come home. They have a lovely house and they are…"

Mary laughed, "Well, I can see you are quite taken with someone or something at that house, so how could I refuse?! I suppose I'd better come and see for myself. Such a kind invitation."

"It's typical of them, Mum, you'll see. Dr Brill said not to stay in here too long. Mum, I'll come and see you tomorrow." Piper smacked her lips together again under the mask and blew her mum a kiss.

Over the next few days Mary became stronger and stronger and the drips were taken away and Piper was allowed to spend longer with her mum. Eventually, Colin was allowed in with Piper.

Mary smiled at them both. "I heard what you've done for me Colin, I wanted to thank you so much."

"Oh, Mrs Milton, it's my pleasure."

"Look, my dad is outside and Dr Brill says you'll be discharged soon. We were wondering if you'd like to stay with us until you are fully fit – as long as you like. We've been delighted to have Piper, and it's nice to have the company."

"Yes, she's been telling me how very kind you've been and what a good cook your dad is. I'll have to up my game when I get out! Are you sure it won't be any trouble."

"No, seriously we'd be delighted. My dad suggested it."

"Okay then, perhaps for a week or so and then we'll return home."

"Well, my dad says you are both welcome for as long as you wish."

Mary smiled at the handsome young man. She paused. She could see what Piper saw in him and smiled again.

Dr Brill was waiting in his office. Piper and Colin went in after knocking at the door.

"Hi, Dr Brill. I hear my mum can come home this week."

"Yes, Piper, and I understand that she'll be staying with you at Colin's home."

"Yes, they've been very kind to me." She looked a little embarrassed as she looked at him. "I'd just like to thank you; thank you for all you've done."

"Well, we were lucky. As you realise, when the Motumixamab failed, we were in trouble but thanks to Colin here…" Suddenly he became more serious. "I remember your mum, Colin, I am sorry we didn't find a donor for her in time."

"Oh, that's not your fault. I'd like to think she's here with me now and pleased that I've been able to help someone like Mary."

A prolonged and awkward silence opened at this point. Piper remembered just in time the contents of the plastic bag she'd brought. "Oh Dr Brill, it's just a little present for you and for Zoe: a couple of bottles of red wine and some chocolates. I want to thank you, both of you, so much." She shook his hand but couldn't resist hugging him again. Zoe blinked back the tears that were forming in the corners of her eyes. She'd hoped and prayed, like never before, for such an outcome and, with luck, it was now within their grasp.

"Are you headed home then, Piper?"

"Yes, Colin's dad will drive us home. I forgot to thank you for laying on the transport all those weeks too."

"Transport?"

"Yes, you know, Brett, the driver."

Piper found herself describing the elderly driver who had been ferrying her about for weeks, who'd turned up come rain or shine when she didn't have money for a taxi, and who always seemed to be waiting to take her home. From the outset, however, Dr Brill's expression revealed that he had no idea who she was referring to.

"We don't have a driver, Piper," he said simply, but now looked a little worried about her as if the strain she had been under for all those weeks had finally taken its toll, or even worse, that there was a bogus driver preying on vulnerable patients!

She laughed with more feeling than he'd anticipated from his quiet reply, as if she was in receipt of more information – much more.

"Is everything all right, Piper?"

"Oh yes, I realise now it must have been a good friend," she offered, as she did her best to reassure him that she was, indeed, sane.

Jeffrey drove them home. Colin and Piper sat in the back of the car. Their hands touched fleetingly as they located their seatbelts. Jeffrey saw in the mirror, his son look quickly at Piper, the smile dancing upon her face just before she looked away.

Chapter 10

Homecoming

A few days later Mary came to stay with the Brogans. As they drove in, she looked at the half-timbered house with the dark bricks not far off a deep chocolate colour, and at the white-framed leaded windows, clay-tiled sweeping roof and the lovely feature bays that extended out into the mature and beautifully kept gardens. Colin and Piper took her cases up to her room. Mary sat with Jeffrey in the kitchen while he made her a cup of tea.

"Jeffrey, you have such a beautiful house."

"Thank you. Colin and I are rattling around here, just the two of us. It's far too big." His voice dipped a little and he moved towards her conspiratorially. "I hope you know, Mary, that we've really enjoyed having Piper here. And it has to be said, Colin especially so…"

She laughed, "Yes, yes I know. I think it's mutual!"

"You know, since she arrived, he gets up for breakfast in the hope of bumping into her."

He joined in with her laughter.

"He's such a lovely lad."

"And she's such a lovely girl"

They laughed again. To Mary, it felt as though she'd not laughed in quite a while.

The following day, an official package was delivered. Mary opened it. It had been sent by the executors of the estate in Ireland and detailed her inheritance, which amounted to just less than a million pounds.

She showed Jeffrey the covering letter. "You know, it's a bequest from a relative I didn't even know I had. We were destitute. I didn't even have money for food, I couldn't pay any bills and we were about to be thrown out of our house. My husband departed and left us with nothing. He wouldn't even reply to my increasingly desperate texts."

"What! He didn't reply to you, not once?" asked Jeffrey with some shock and incredulity. "And you were married for, what, twenty years! What a …" He shut his mouth quickly, thinking that he was about to say too much. She nodded, acknowledging her agreement and his restraint.

"I didn't even have money for a taxi. It was a good job that driver showed up just when he did, as I'd never have got there. Piper was so good. She spent all her birthday money and then walked up the road to get a summer job in the bakery, starting at 5am every day, and still did her best to come with me to hospital. Of course, it was all too much for her but it did at least allow us to buy some food. And that is why you see her at breakfast: to her it's the middle of the day!"

"Mary, she's quite an impressive young woman."

"And just look what Colin did. He is no less impressive, I think."

Their conversation was curtailed as Piper and Colin entering; they'd been for a bike ride.

Piper was in the hallway taking off her shoes as Mary called her in to the sitting room. "Piper, take a look at this." She showed her daughter the paperwork. "We are financially secure now thanks to relatives I didn't know existed. We won't have to worry about losing the roof over our heads or unpaid bills. I can settle our affairs quickly."

Mary knew that Piper had been worrying about their financial situation and was keen to reassure her. Mary changed the topic of conversation. "Say, Piper, we were just talking about Brett. Even though you say Dr Brill said they didn't have a driver, who do you think he was? I was wondering, do you think he …"

Piper laughed, before her mother could finish her sentence, "Mum, we'll probably never know, trust me." She wondered whether she would see the mysterious and ever-present elderly chap again. She suddenly had a feeling, deep within, that it was only a matter of time. Moreover, in that moment, she realised that, somehow and somewhere, she'd heard his voice before – even before he turned up that day to take them to St Catherine's for their first appointment.

The following day, and a few days late, Piper started back at school. She joined the sixth form at a nearby college. Colin insisted on taking her and bringing her back and said that he hoped that he wouldn't destroy her street cred by being in the same car.

Piper informed him, keeping a straight face, that she thought this was unlikely to happen. Notwithstanding this, her friends quickly spotted her exiting the little red car and curiosity soon spiked.

For the most part, Mary was content to stay in the large house with the beautiful gardens. She was especially content to be talking with Jeffrey and, on many occasions, they'd look at the clock only to be surprised at how much time had passed. He even accompanied her while she took walks in the extensive grounds of the house. Eventually, they started journeying further afield to the local woods and the park. Slowly but surely, her strength returned and she helped with the cooking and also took part in many of the jobs in the house.

"You know, Colin is starting at Cambridge in a couple of weeks." Jeffrey said one day.

"Oh yes, I'm sorry, Jeffrey, would you like us to move out? We have both taken advantage of your kindness for so long."

Jeffrey laughed. "Oh no, that's not what I was about to say. Please stay…for as long as you want. I mean it. Perhaps I should simply say – please stay, both of you. What I was going to say is that I have a feeling that Colin will come home most weekends. Is that acceptable?"

Mary smiled. "Oh, it is to me, but I'm sure she wouldn't want to intrude on his social life or his studies."

"Truth be told, I think he'd kill me if I didn't try every trick in the book to get you both to stay."

"Look, are you sure we aren't intruding?"

For years now, since my wife died, Colin and I have been leading a non-life. Existing, not living. Maybe it's time to do stuff that living folk do, like go for walks, have meals out and go to the pictures. Whatever you feel you'd be comfortable with?

"What, me?"

"Yes you, and of course Piper. As I said, I think Colin will be home each weekend."

"Okay, why not. If we take it slow and if we get in the way then please, please just say. I think maybe I should help with some of the running costs and of course, if I am not offending, continue to help you in the kitchen and around the house."

He smiled, "Okay, we can maybe talk about that, but we do love having you both here. I retired after selling my business after my wife died. Money will never be an issue and I suspect now the same applies for you too. Think about what you will be comfortable with. I'm not going to put pressure on you apart from telling you that you are welcome here, of course. Now that you have settled the mortgage on your house, you can return there as often as you wish or rent it out or even sell it - whatever works for you."

"Sell it?"

"I suppose I am saying, maybe think about it when the time is right for you and when you are ready, we can discuss some of the other issues."

"I also have an estate in Ireland that I need to go and take a look at. They say it's a bit run down and needs some work. I couldn't persuade you to come and look it over with me, could I?"

"Oh yes, very easily. That's just up my street. I used to have my own surveying company so I think, without blowing my own trumpet, I'd be really useful. We could go as soon as you feel strong enough to travel. Just say the word."

"I will, I promise and…"

Just then the doorbell rang.

Jeffrey went to the door but called Mary a few moments later. He'd invited the gentleman into the hall. It was someone he didn't recognise, but he suspected he knew exactly who the chap was as soon as the door opened. Not wanting to eavesdrop, Jeffrey withdrew to his study and quietly closed the door, leaving them to talk. But somehow, the door opened despite his closing it carefully.

"Oh Mary! Am I glad to see you."

"George!"

"Look, Mary, I've been a complete idiot. Our neighbours told me where to find you. I've made a terrible mistake. I realised I was about to throw twenty years away; twenty good years. I'm here to ask you, is there any way I can come back to you and to Piper?"

"Why, George? Why now? After all this time."

"I made a mistake, Mary. A big mistake and I regret it more than anything."

She looked at his unshaven and dishevelled appearance. Then she looked over his shoulder at the blue car in the drive. Suddenly, women's intuition kicked in as she wondered if he'd been sleeping in his car.

"She's thrown you out!"

His abject embarrassment told her all she needed to know.

“Well, not exactly, but I thought it was time to come back. How about it?’

“Look, George, Piper and I have been through so much and we came through because of some wonderful people and friends who have helped us in ways that we can never repay. They have shown us what real friends do and, sadly, you were not present to even learn from that.”

“I accept I’ve made mistakes. I now know through it all, Mary, that I still love you and that we should be a proper family again.”

“That’s the thing, George. I realised that, although it’s been twenty years, you *never* loved me. Maybe it was a reflex or a gamble or an urge you felt you had to go with. I can now see that you were never there for me and I think you weren’t there for our special little girl either. I blame myself for not seeing this. I should have asked you, asked you years ago, rather than wait for you to move on. I guess I am as much to blame as you. Maybe it was my illness, whatever, but I can see clearly now, George, and I can see that what we had wasn’t very much at all. Your leaving has done us both a favour and I suppose in time you will see that too.”

“No, that’s ridiculous, Mary. I do love you and of course, Piper. Let’s go home, the three of us, and we can put all this behind us and I can prove it to you.”

She gently touched his arm but her words slowed so that she and he could be clear. “I’m sorry, George, but Piper and I have moved on. We are now very different people and I realise with some regret, but also looking at things honestly, you are no longer a part of our lives.

“You can see Piper whenever you wish, provided she wants to see you. You will need to telephone her to seek her views and I promise not to influence her. But I can’t and won’t make her if she does not wish to see you. I’m sure it can’t be lost, even on you, that you chose to depart just as she was preparing for her GCSE exams and it’s no thanks to you that she did as well as she did. I’ll also be filing for a divorce and, given the time we have been apart, this should now be just a formality.”

George suddenly looked around at the magnificent house as if noticing it for the first time.

“What are you even doing here? Are you having an affair? Who are these people?”

"Oh, George, that's a little rich coming from you! I might add that it is no longer your business who or what these people, as you put it, are but I can say that *these people* are our friends who I realise have come, within a few days, to mean so much, both to me and to Piper. I'm not quite sure, to give you more explanation than you perhaps deserve, just where it will lead and for how long, but I do know that I am happy here with some very fine people and I believe that Piper is too. I'll be here for as long as that situation persists or for as long as we are wanted.

"I'm sorry, George, I really am, it gives me no pleasure to see your relationship fail, and I certainly don't want to gloat or to say things to spite you. This is the simple truth of the matter; there is no way back for me and I suspect not for Piper either – at least not for the moment. I've never seen Piper happier than she is now. I promise to tell her you called and if you let me have your new number, I'll pass it to her."

"Mary, you are making a terrible mistake."

She laughed involuntarily, "No, I think for the first time in my life I can see things clearly. Going back to what we had or what we thought we had would be the mistake."

It was only then that another thought came to her as she stood there. She remembered the young woman, the brilliant one, with the agile mind who taught Physics. She recalled a class that had been enrolled one year, none of whom seemed to be able to grasp the elegant complexities of Simple harmonic motion. She'd stood there before them and had gone through it line by line until each and every one of them not only understood it, but also was able to calculate the formulae that lay behind it. That woman had been bedazzled by a man who'd insisted that the things that he'd told her, and that being with him, was far more important than her career and the life she'd known and been very good at. How trusting and naïve she had been. He'd said much over the years, but demonstrated little. And then, one day, he'd got bored. It was time for that woman, who still resided within, to make a return.

Mary broke eye contact and focussed firmly on the front door of solid oak. He was forced to accept that the conversation was over as was his marriage and things had most definitely moved on for his wife, the ex-professor of Physics, and daughter. He realised just before Mary looked away that he'd never noticed in all their years together the colour of her eyes – pale amber. It seemed they would now be lost to him forever. He left through the door as she held it open, without looking at him. She gently closed the door, turned and rested her back and head against it with some relief and the certainty of both her words and actions that day.

In the study, out of sight, Jeffrey gave a little smile. He never knew what had made the door open in that way and he hadn't meant to intrude on their conversation and yet he could only be pleased that he had.

He couldn't help but feel that although the future was not a given, both mother and daughter would be better with him and Colin and hopefully, although he'd make it clear they could come and go as they wished, they would prefer to remain where they were. He now knew that her thoughts were not dissimilar to his own.

Colin came in. He'd been out for a run.

"Dad, who was that man driving away?"

Mary spoke before Jeffrey could form words.

"Oh, it's someone from mine and Piper's past and not our future." Colin guessed very quickly from this who the gentleman was driving the dirty and uncared for Porsche. He nodded and glanced at his dad. His dad returned his smile and quickly winked at him as Mary's gaze was elsewhere. Colin nodded again as a conclusion came to him and without further words, went upstairs to shower.

Chapter 11

The Man

It was late afternoon, Colin went out to pick Piper up from school. Sitting in the passenger seat, she seemed preoccupied as if she'd been thinking things through and was keen to get something off her chest. He returned her smile but otherwise waited for her to speak.

"Colin, it's so kind of you to ferry me about. You know, you don't have to do this; I can get the bus."

"I know, but the car was on the drive and I just looked up and saw the time."

She laughed. "All the other girls keep asking me who that handsome guy is who drops me off and picks me up. They all want your number."

"And what do you tell them?"

"Well, I know you won't want to be pestered when you are going off to university soon, so I tell them that you're spoken for. Is that alright?"

"In that case, we'd better make it look authentic, I suppose."

Suddenly, he leant towards her and kissed her.

The shy and introverted young woman who had finished her GCSEs that summer, and had come home looking for a quiet break from school before she started at sixth form, was very different from the one who now sat next to that handsome young man. Yes, she'd experienced much sadness and loss, just in seeing her dad depart, even before her mother's illness had taken her to death's door. And yet, the young woman who emerged from that was not only grateful to have come through but also someone who was stronger and, most importantly, had realised that life could be fleeting and sometimes, happy events had to be grasped without hesitation. It was this young woman who now spoke.

"I don't think everyone saw. Could we do that again?" She leant towards him and kissed him.

They both smiled. “That should leave them in no doubt. Of course, they’ll all be dead jealous now. Let’s see now;” she counted on her fingers, “car picking me up, boy friend, handsome bloke. I think that’s the order of importance in their eyes.”

“Oh, *boyfriend* now, am I?”

It wasn’t quite as she’d intended but she recovered quickly, “Well, only if you’d like.” Her big eyes surveyed him carefully.

He smiled just as he returned her steady, open gaze, “Just how could I say no?” He kissed her again.

Just then, Piper reflected a stunning smile back at him, but in that moment remembered something that she now knew was really important. She said, “It’s time. Colin, I need to do something. When we get in, would you be able to take me to the local tip?”

“Yes, of course, but why?”

“Oh, I can’t really explain but you are welcome to come along. It’s best if you see it with your own eyes. You’ll understand much more that way and I can then try to answer your questions as best I can.”

Colin was now intrigued and full of questions, but he decided to simply go along with Piper’s request. They reached home. Both son and daughter peeped into the orangery and Jeffrey was in animated conversation with Mary.

“Oh no, look at those two,” she smiled as she nodded towards them, “You’ll never be able to get rid of us, you know that don’t you!”

“I was kind of hoping that would be so.”

“I need to get the case down.”

“The old case that you brought with you?”

She nodded.

“Okay, I’ll come and help you.”

Colin stood at the door while she grabbed the case from her room. There on the bed, he saw the unicorn lying on her pillow.

“Oh, what a fabulous unicorn. Was that a present from someone? It looks just like the lucky charm on my key ring.” He held out his key ring for her inspection.

“Yes, they are from the same person.”

“What? How do you know that?”

"We are going to meet him, now."

"What?! At the tip! How do you know this person, whoever he is, will be there?"

She smiled the smile that was becoming much more frequent these days. It seemed to shine from her face like warm sunshine establishing itself after the passage of a particularly dark and severe winter. A smile that he now knew had become part of his own happiness and his life and he suspected that of his father's too. More than this, it was a smile of confidence and yet one that remained demure.

She held out her hand. "Come with me, and you will see. I'm not sure you'll believe me but it's time to return something very special. And trust me, he'll be there."

Colin nodded, thinking that he could never foresee a time when he couldn't or wouldn't believe her or trust her.

They drove to the tip and Colin helped Piper remove the case from the car.

There, waiting for them was the balding chap with the corduroy trousers barely meeting around his middle.

Colin looked at the elderly gentleman. "Have I seen you somewhere before?"

Piper laughed. "Oh yes, most certainly." She grabbed the elderly gentleman's hand as if she was never going to let it go, now that she had secured it.

"It's you isn't it?" Pauses came as she tried to prioritise so many thoughts. "It was you all along, wasn't it? You, and always you!"

The old chap nodded. "Yes, and my friends." He nodded again and looked at her, "Nice hair, Piper."

"I want to thank you so much. I want to thank you from the bottom of my heart. I'm sorry I nearly threw the case away. I'm sorry I doubted you, or your case."

"The case is fine. I can tell you that we, all of us, were frightened. We also had doubts and it was such a close call. You were so brave, Piper." Eyes of china blue, made a little cloudy with age, surveyed hers that were bright and clear. He smiled.

"Thank you for all this," she moved her hands apart as if trying to represent the enormity of what he'd done. He smiled again; the china blue became a little moist as well as cloudy.

"My mum is so much better, but I think you know that don't you?"

The old man nodded again and chuckled.

Colin started nodding too; he now understood just a little more. "May I ask, have you a big dog?" The elderly chap smiled and nodded. "Ah yes, Barney, my friend, too," as he patted the red case that Piper had handed to him.

"Is this case yours?" Colin asked as he pointed to the dull red case with golden zips that now glowed in the fading sun.

"Yes, in a manner of speaking. But we lend it to people who have need of it." He nodded towards the other side of the tip. "Like that young woman down there." He drew their attention to a blue car that had just pulled up. "She has a cake shop and bakery that is about to close. If it does fail, so many will come to harm. We can help her."

"Piper, Colin could I ask you?" he nodded again to the young woman who had just got out of the car.

Piper nodded, "Don't tell me, you can bake as well!"

He chuckled, "Well, my friend can bake a lovely Victoria sponge."

"I don't doubt it." She took the case as he offered it back. "Yes, yes, of course. Colin, would you come with me?" She turned to look at the mysterious elderly gent. "I have so many questions of you, Brett. Only, it's not really Brett, is it?"

"No, I thought your mum might prefer that name."

Piper laughed. She squeezed the elderly man's hand a little harder and then let go, meaning it not only to underline her sincere gratitude but also hoping it was to be a down payment on all the questions she wanted to ask as soon as she'd passed on the case.

"Don't go away, we'll be right back. I want to ask you so much."

He chuckled.

She and Colin walked down to the young woman with the blue car, trailing the red case behind them.

Piper spoke with the young baker for a while. She knew that her explanation about the case would also fill in some of the details for Colin who had many questions. Although the cake shop owner remained a little puzzled, she accepted the case.

Piper had some final suggestions: "Please don't put the case anywhere cold or dark, will you? It likes to have company and be in the warmth and the light."

The lady with the blue car laughed. "No, alright, I won't; I promise."

"And don't forget to pat it or stroke it when you talk to it."

"I will!"

"In return, it will help you in ways you cannot yet imagine. Just give it a day or two. And one final thing, you'll know when to return it."

Piper hugged her and wished her luck. Colin shook her hand and also wished her well.

"But who do I return it to?" asked the shop owner.

"The elderly gentleman, we were just talking to, he's…he's…over there."

She and Colin turned. They looked for the old man who was nowhere to be seen. They wondered, as many had done before and many would do so again, just where he might have gone, but they did so in vain.

"He's gone!" she said.

"Where did he go to?" wondered Colin.

"Now, that's just one of the things I was going to ask him!"

Piper and Colin walked back to where he'd parked his car.

"So, are you are saying that's a Magic Case?" he asked.

"Oh yes. Do you think I am mad?"

"No, I suppose I'm wondering why I am not more surprised. So, you pass it on when it's helped you? How do you know when?"

"Oh, I think you just know. When it is time to share the Magic."

Colin laughed, "I'm not sure I can take it all in."

Piper laughed too and held his hand.

"Tell me about it!"

She held his hand, firmly. "I'm thinking that I will never get answers to all those questions I was going to ask. Maybe that's how it all works and some things must remain forever as part of the mystery. At least I got to thank him from the bottom of my heart. Maybe it's simply time for us to begin a new adventure."

"I was hoping you'd say that, Piper Milton." He kissed her.

THE END